JUST A LITTLE TALK

Just a Little Talk

WITH A NEW INTRODUCTION BY THE AUTHOR

Anthony Crescio

FRESHImage Press

Published by FRESHImage Press, LLC
www.freshimage.org

Illustrations by Klayton Kindt

ISBN: 979-8-9853839-0-4

Second Printing, 2021
First Printing, 2011

To my mom and dad,
for getting me through the tough times.

And in memory of Pugs.

Contents

Acknowledgments

Putting a book together is no small task. At FRESHImage Press we are a small family team that worked hard to bring you this new printing of *Just A Little Talk* about a decade after its first publication.

First of all, a debt of gratitude is owed to my parents, John & Irma Crescio. Besides giving me the gift of life, they have been the biggest cheerleaders of that life, even when there wasn't much to cheer for. As if this wasn't enough, when *Just A Little Talk* was first released, my mom did much of the distribution herself. This time around she served as an extra pair of eyes on the manuscript, helping us to catch any slip ups that got passed us the first time around. Thank you both!

Second, my faithful and meticulous in-house editor, my sister, Alex Cooper. Alex, has done everything from help me put college applications together to serving as an extra set of eyes on nearly everything I have written over the past decade or so. She helped edit the first printing of *Just A Little Talk* and was on board for the project again this time. Your help can never be repaid!

Finally, my wife, Vanessa Crescio. Vanessa bears the distinct burden of being married to a dreamer, and yet, somehow, she always finds it in herself to be supportive of those dreams. Since we were married just over five years ago,

Vanessa has patiently listened to ideas, reviewed, critiqued and edited countless papers, and now this book. To say that you are a blessing in my life is to say too little, the presence of God's goodness and love you are in my life is beyond description.

Introduction

Midway upon the journey of our life
I found myself within a forest dark,
For the straightforward pathway had been lost.
>   Dante, *The Divine Comedy*, Canto 1.1-3

The words above by the great Italian poet, Dante, describe much more eloquently the situation I found myself in just over a decade ago which would eventually give birth to the book you now hold in your hands. In fact, it is not incorrect to say that the very text in some sense records the process of my rebirth, an effort to regain the straightforward path that had been lost, the words on the page marking the contractions by which God drew me out of the darkness of the destruction wrought by my own sin and ignorance into the light of a new life in Him (1 Peter 2:9).

How did I arrive at such a place? The same way we all do I suppose. A life driven by self-centered desires chasing one fleeting pleasure after another in the futile hope that some measure of happiness might be obtained. Yet it never is. Even temporal goods which bring us happinesses of all sorts become poisonous when placed before love of God, the only source of ultimate Happiness which all other happinesses, if they are to be authentic, must be directed toward. And I in the midst of restless youth could not even take solace in the knowledge that the things I pursued were goods taken to extremes. Instead, the focus was the satisfying of a consumptive ego by any means within reach. And so, in one act of defiance after another, I grasped at objects of desire one after another until like Adam, I fell headlong into the center of my own pride where I found nothing except my own pain.

Looking back now, it couldn't have been any other way. A self-centered life, however ostensibly lived in the company of others, necessarily leads to destruction of some kind. Self-centeredness almost always leads to varying levels of self-destruction. And, generally speaking, the degree of self-destruction is related to the degree of destruction one brings upon those closest to them. In my case, self-centeredness not only led to self-destruction but to the loss of a life very close and dear to me to whom this book is dedicated together with my parents, who, more than any others, helped me bear that immense weight of loss, guilt, shame and distress in the wake of this tragedy.

On the pages of this book, you will find many allusions to those without whose assistance I would never have emerged from the darkness that surrounded me at that time and to whom I am forever grateful. In the midst of the dark night in which I lay praying for divine intervention to stop the pain, their faces become the very presence of God to me, the bearers of an amazing grace of which I will never be worthy. Disguised in the presence of many family members and close friends, the Hound of Heaven eventually chased me down. And it is through them, together with the healing grace of the

Church's sacraments, that the God who made me began to re-make me, to paraphrase the great St. Augustine of Hippo.[1]

As light dawned in the darkness, my mind began to awaken as from a long slumber, ravenous to consume any-thing and everything that would both provide the answers to the questions I now had and the nourishment necessary for the long and arduous journey I knew lay immediately before me. My list of questions included the usual ones. How had I gotten so lost? Why had God allowed my own situation to get so bad that others now suffered along with me? And finally, who was I now, and what future could I possibly have in the wake of this tragedy?

One day I stumbled upon a copy of C. S. Lewis's *Mere Christianity* on one of my parents' bookshelves. Placed there by the hand of someone else in the house, it now seems as though it was placed there by the hand of Divine Providence Itself. With great ardor I read through those pages, loving every sentence. Therein I found myself the subject of a res-cue mission carried out by the very Son of God, who Lewis so memorably described as landing in disguise in enemy-oc-cupied territory to carry out the great work of salvation.[2] Not long after I would realize that the enemy-occupied territory was within no less than without.

That realization came by way of another of Lewis' texts. Having been captivated by *Mere Christianity*, I went looking for another one of Lewis' works. I acquired a copy of *The Problem of Pain*, and life was never the same again. Still strug-gling mightily to make sense of the pain I was feeling, I found Lewis speaking directly to me as he described pain as God's megaphone. Being in the midst of immense emotional and psychological pain, the words jumped off the page at me. At that moment, I felt as though God must be calling to me through the pain I felt. Reading the words over again in their full context, what was experienced as relief as I read over the words initially now aroused the sense of shame and guilt that lay deep within. For here is what I read:

> We can rest contentedly in our sins and in our stupidities; and anyone who has watched gluttons shoveling down the most exquisite foods as if they did not know what they were eating, will admit that we can ignore even pleasure. But pain insists upon being attended to. God whispers to us in our pleasures, speaks in our conscience, but shouts in our pain: it is His megaphone to rouse a deaf world.[3]

I had ignored my stupidities and rested contentedly in my sins for a long while. I even ignored the pleasures I experienced as after a time they too lost any taste and became a bland diet. But there was no mistaking the pain. Its bitterness had left a taste in my mouth that could never be rinsed out.

There are innumerable ways we humans try to deal with pain, not many of them good. Most of our responses to pain of whatever sort are various forms of an instinctual flight from pain. You see Dominic momentarily consider this type of escapism in the very first chapter of this book. Yet something stops him, grace. Without articulating it, Dominic senses a deep truth about such escapism. Fr. William Kane, S.J., explains it this way:

As with so many of our blundering human efforts, we move here in a vicious circle, running into evils through our flight from evils. It is at least possible that our negative paradise-hunting may at times defeat itself, and may carry us farther away from paradise. The problem of pain can easily become the problem of choice between a small misery of present pain and a huge misery of future pain, either in this life or in eternity.[4]

From the very night that the tragedy had taken place, I had tried to flee from the pain I felt in various ways characterized best by the stages of grief and loss described by psychologists: denial, anger at myself, bargaining with God (up to the point of asking Him to divinely intervene so as to make the pain end completely and permanently), and depression. The only thing I had not done was the only thing that would open up the future, accept the situation I had gotten myself in and address it. I knew the pain I experienced was my own doing, it was no secret. And as I read further into Lewis' *The Problem of Pain*, I had this truth reaffirmed to me along with advice for finding a path forward.

Lewis describes three functions of pain in his text. The first is that pain dispels the illusion that all is well with our current state. The crushing of this illusion opens up two possibilities, rebellion or conversion.[5] By the grace of God I was in no shape, or situation, where further rebellion was possible. I had used up all my rebellious energy in acquiring the pain I now experienced. And because I had, I also realized that the second of Lewis' statements concerning the function of pain was true as well: that pain shatters the illusion of self-sufficiency.[6] With the first two functions of pain having been at work on me for some time, which I now realized in retrospect, it was a providential moment for me to read what Lewis names as the third operation of pain: that pain is symptomatic of a life totally surrendered to God.[7]

Sufficiently familiar now with the pain which calls to conversion, I felt ready to endure the pain of surrendering to God. As a cradle Catholic who had spent a good bit of my life up to then avoiding living my faith fully, I knew my father was right when he asked me to avail myself of the healing grace of the Sacrament of Reconciliation. The darkness of the confessional was as bright as day compared to the darkness within my soul, and as I knelt there choking back tears with all the emotional energy left within me, I accused myself of my horrific crime against God and neighbor. In response, I heard Our Lord speak the healing words of forgiveness to me through the mouth of His minister. Sweeter words were never spoken.

And so it began. To my steady diet of reading, by God's grace I added a fairly intense regimen of prayer. And as I prayed and learned, and learned and prayed, my basement bedroom transformed from one type of cell to another. On the wall hung the same crucifix that had been in my bedroom since I was a little boy. But now seen with the eyes of faith reopened by grace, the image of Our Lord's outstretched arms on the instrument of torture upon which He won our salvation for love of us, spoke to me directly, convicting and convincing me of a very deep reality. I could not have articulated then what I experienced as I gazed upon that throne of love. After years of study, I believe that what I sensed then is best described by the theologian Hans Urs von Balthasar:

> When man encounters the love of God in Christ, not only does he experience what genuine love is, but he is also confronted with the undeniable fact that he, a selfish sinner, does not himself possess true love. He experiences two things at once: the finitude of the creature's love and its sinful frigidity.[8]

Life is the great classroom of love. Only by God's grace do we learn to love as we ought, do we begin to love in the manner we have been created to love. Gazing upon the throne of the cross, the throne of love, we come to realize that to be fully human means to give oneself completely, to love God and neighbor as oneself without remainder. Our primary exemplar who is at once the Way by which we grow in our ability to love rightly and the End in which our love is completed is Christ. In the ultimate sacrifice of love alone do we see the purpose for which the human person was created, to be a complete gift of love in unity with Him to Our Heavenly Father by the power of the Holy Spirit working within us. Part of the tragedy of human life in a fallen world is that learning how to love in this way, growing to full maturity as a human person, is always accompanied by some form of pain, as we saw Lewis suggest above.

The reasons for this are countless, but the most basic is this: when we take up our own crosses and follow Christ, what we leave behind is the old self. And leaving the old self behind is painful because we have come to love that self, however false and imperfect it is, as our true self. Lewis again, here, provides us with vivid imagery to exemplify what we are talking about, this time in *The Great Divorce*.

Within this beautiful novel, Lewis depicts those who have not yet had their love perfected as ghosts, less substantial beings than those who have been filled with the Love that Is God to perfection and who now live eternally in Heaven. One of these ghosts is a man who enters the story with what looks like a lizard on his shoulder.[9] The lizard-like creature represents the vice of lust. Soon after entering the story, the ghostly man encounters an angel, who offers to get rid of the grotesque creature who clings to him so tightly. The ghost says he would rather not trouble the angel or have the creature destroyed. Soon it becomes apparent that it is the ghost who is clinging to the lizard, not vice versa, for the ghost tells the angel that killing the lizard would do no less than kill him.[10] After a back-and-forth, the ghost comes to realize that to remain attached to the lizard in the end would prevent him from living anyhow, and the angel sets to work. The ghost cries out in pain, and to Lewis' amazement, who recounts the whole episode for us, the ghost is transformed into a man and far from being destroyed, the lizard is transformed into a beautiful stallion with mane and tail of gold.[11] Now transformed, the man and horse thank the angel and ride off together until "they vanished, bright themselves, into the rose-brightness of that everlasting morning."[12]

Like the ghost in Lewis' *The Great Divorce*, we shrink from the action that will bring us healing because healing comes by way of pain, be it momentary or prolonged. What Lewis so wonderfully depicts in that scene is the great truth that the act of leaving that self behind is always experienced as a type of death. For in truth, whatever it is that we need healing from, whether it be a vice such as lust as it was for the ghost in *The Great Divorce*, another of the deadly gang of seven, a disordered relationship, an addiction of any sort, or the pursuit of worldly goods, fame, honor, titles or wealth, leaving them and our disordered love of them behind, is a type of death, specifically the crucifixion of the old self, enslaved to sin, as St. Paul says (Romans 6:6).

These truths, so wonderfully related to us in Scripture, written about by the great minds of the Great Tradition, and depicted by artists and writers like Lewis, are truths I began to sense then, but had not the education to articulate well. What I did have were the practices of my faith which I had learned from childhood and an immense amount of free time on my hands. And so, I began sitting down for some time each day and writing this little book.

How to Read This Book

One of the most beautiful prayers of the Catholic Tradition and one which I gravitated towards given the situation I found myself in is *The Way of the Cross* (or *The Stations of the Cross*). Enabling the one who prays them the ability to focus on each moment of Our Lord's Passion and thereby to draw one deeper into that saving event drew me to the Stations. I knew then that the "straightforward path" that I had once lost and upon which I had to traverse if I were to find healing, was nothing else except the road up to Calvary, traveled in unity with Christ. And thus, as I sat down to write something that I might share with others in order to help them deal with and overcome the pain and suffering that they faced, this prayer loomed large in my mind and eventually became part of the structure of the book.

Accordingly, I think there are a couple of ways that one could read this book and derive some benefit from it. First, one could read it straightforwardly as the novel that it is. If so, I think you will find some helpful insights imaginatively expressed that can help you along your own personal journey of discipleship.

Secondly, you could read this as a reflection on your own life's journey of Christian discipleship. I gave the name Dominic to the main character for this very reason. The name "Dominic" means "of the Lord." And so, as I wrote, I wanted each and every person who wants to live as one "of the Lord's" to be able to place themselves in Dominic's shoes and with him move towards healing in their own lives.

Finally, a third way of reading this book was suggested by a now deceased beloved priest friend of my family, Fr. Stanley Baranowski. After reading the book, Fr. Stan suggested that it could be read as a reflection on the *Stations of the Cross* themselves. Even though this was not my initial intent, I think he was right, and if I had a suggestion to make, I think this the most fruitful way of reading this little work. The book can be read in this fashion at any time, of course, but is perhaps most appropriate to do as a Lenten reflection or devotion.

If you choose this option, you could perhaps begin by making an examination of conscience before reading the book. What are you struggling with most in your life right now? What is that thing or situation that is keeping you from leaving everything behind and following Christ? As you move through the novel you will move through the Stations of Our Lord's Passion, and as you do, reflect upon and imitate what you see there as Dominic does. Allow yourself to express your guilt and recognize your shortcomings, but also to take notice of the blessings that surround you even amidst the struggles you face. Slowly, you will make your trek up Calvary, and there, with Dominic, you will realize that though this is perhaps the most difficult journey you will ever make, there is nothing else you would rather give your life to, for in reflecting on Our Lord's Passion, you will find yourself falling in love with the One Who loved you first. It is in this process of falling in love that you will find healing, and come one step closer to living the fullness of a human life, a life of loving self-gift.

Whatever way you, the reader, choose to utilize this book, I pray that it draw you one step closer to the person God created you to be. And I ask that you, in return, pray for its author as well, for he still struggles to stay on "the straightforward path" and his own remaking by God's grace is far from complete.

Anthony Crescio
The Solemnity of the Immaculate Conception
December 8, 2021

1. ^Augustine of Hippo, Letter 231.6, in *Letters* II/4, trans. Roland J. Teske, S.J. (Hyde Park, New City Press, 2005), 122.

2. ^C. S. Lewis, *Mere Christianity* (San Francisco, Harper Collins, 2001), 46.

3. ^C. S. Lewis, *The Problem of Pain* (New York, Harper Collins, 1996), 91.

4. ^William Kane, S.J., *Paradise Hunters* (St. Louis, B Herder Book Co., 1946), 187.

5. ^C. S. Lewis, *The Problem of Pain*, 93.

6. ^Ibid., 94.

7. ^Ibid., 97-98.

8. ^Hans Urs von Balthasar, *Love Alone Is Credible* trans. D. C. Schindler (San Francisco, Ignatius Press, 2004), 61.

9. ^C. S. Lewis, *The Great Divorce* (New York, Harper Collins, 1973), 106.

10. ^Ibid., 109.

11. ^Ibid., 111.

12. ^Ibid., 112.

Prologue

S o what's our ETA looking like?" Eddy asked as he pulled a pack of cigarettes out of his inside coat pocket.

"Oh, a little less than an hour I'd say," Dominic answered, taking a brief pause from singing along with the radio. "Let me get one of those." He held out his hand to Eddy.

"Man, I gotta spoon feed you everything," Eddy said with a smirk, handing Dominic a cigarette.

"Hey, easy there. If I remember correctly, I lent you the money for the pack, but I could be wrong. It has been a long night," Dominic added sarcastically.

"Ooh, ouch," Eddy said as he began to laugh. "You got me there."

"Well, what can I say, buddy?" Dominic said, looking over at his friend in the passenger seat. "Sometimes you make it so easy."

Taking jabs at each other was a central part of the relationship the two best friends shared with each other. It was part of a friendship that began way back in kindergarten and had lasted the better part of two decades. Since kindergarten, the two had faced many things together in their young lives, good and bad. The end of high school saw the two move off to college together, only to see them move right back home

1

to Riverdale to work for Dominic's dad. The relationship the two shared was more that of brothers than of friends, and even though the two weren't very open with their emotions, they both knew the brotherly love that existed between them.

Tonight would be no different than countless others the two had shared. Partying until the sun came up and then paying for it the next day with splitting headaches that reduced their conversations to whispers. At least that was the plan.

That was the plan until an easy left turn proved to be more than Dominic could negotiate under the influence.

"Hang on, Eddy," Dominic said, tension in his voice as he desperately tried to regain control of the vehicle.

"Oh crap," Eddy said as the rear end of the car traded places with the front on the road. The sound of squealing tires split the silence of the night as the car spun out of control.

Dominic watched in slow motion as the steering wheel was jerked out of his hands. Was this happening? Was this real? The sound of shattering glass once again brought the action to full speed for Dominic, and with a crack, he felt a sharp pain in his leg as he was lifted out of the driver's seat. *Oh my God* was the last thought that came to Dominic's head before he awoke to sheer terror and darkness, complete darkness.

What happened? Dominic thought as he came to. *And where's Eddy?* "Eddy! Eddy!" Dominic screamed over and over, but the only sound that returned his calls was silence.

Chapter One

Riverdale looked much the same to Dominic as he stepped off the bus downtown. It felt good to have the sunshine upon his face again. People were rushing all around him, but Dominic needed to just take a moment and let the reality that he was now a free man sink in a bit. He had gotten off the bus downtown so he could have some time to walk around and gather his thoughts before he went home to see his family. As Dominic stood in the middle of the sidewalk and took in the old and some new sights, he wondered if anybody recognized him here anymore.

The neighborhood was still all too familiar to him. Although things mostly looked the same, it was apparent that things had changed with time. Wally's Auto Supply had been replaced by a chain auto parts store, and the vacant lot next to it where Dominic had gathered with his friends so many nights growing up was now home to a hair salon. As Dominic made his way up the street, the familiar smell of fresh pastries coming from Edna's Café was comforting to him. Edna's had been a fixture of the downtown area for as long as Dominic could remember. As Riverdale grew over the course of Dominic's lifetime, larger chain stores took the place of small mom-and-pop shops, but the place that always stood the test of time was Edna's. Of course the fact that Edna Miller, the café's owner, was one of the sweetest ladies in town certainly helped. Her smile and cheery demeanor kept her customers coming back. As Dominic walked past and looked in the window, Edna waved and gave him a smile. As Dominic waved back, he recognized the other customers stop and stare at him as if he had come back from the dead.

As he continued to make his way up the street, the thought crossed his mind that his family would appear the same way. He wondered if there was any place for him there anymore. Though his family had been great about visiting and writing while he was away, it was impossible for things to remain the same between them. He just couldn't be Dominic in prison. The need to constantly look over his shoulder and question whether or not he could trust every person he came into contact with changed Dominic's view of people. For all practical purposes, for the last eight years, Dominic's former self ceased to exist. His time at Red Valley Prison had simply made him inmate number 566945. He had gone in a young, twenty-one-year-old man, and while at twenty-nine he was by no means an old man, the man that walked past the windows of the stores and cafés wasn't the same man he remembered seeing in the windows eight years ago.

A red car rushed past, and the tires squealed as it turned the corner in front of him. Immediately the hairs on the back of his neck stood at attention, and shivers went up his spine. A cold sensation came over his body. He didn't think certain sounds would be such a trigger for him anymore. "Some things never go away," he said to himself.

He continued his walk and soon came upon The Watering

Hole. It had been his favorite place to meet up with his friends and put home a couple of cold ones after a hard day at work. He stood out front looking in, thinking about going inside. He was sure he would see some friendly faces that he hadn't seen in a while. Besides, what could be the harm? After all, he hadn't had a drop in almost nine years. He had been locked up so long, he owed it to himself to stop in and have a few, he thought. At least it would take the edge off before he had to go home.

He walked toward the front door and reached out to pull the handle. Just then, he heard another sound that he was sure would always give him goose bumps. Sirens blared off in the distance, and he pulled back his hand from the door.

"What am I doing?" he said to himself. "How could I forget?" He was walking toward the same thing that took him away from everything he loved. How could he forget what led to that tragedy and the sheer terror of that bitter-cold December night, when his life as he'd known it and all the plans he'd had for his future ceased to exist in the blink of an eye. No buzz would be worth risking that kind of pain again.

He continued his walk down the street. As the sirens continued to sound, every gut-wrenching memory of that night began to well up inside of him. It had been almost nine years, and he could still recall every sight and sound of that night of hell. Feeling he needed to clear his head, he began to look for a quiet place to sit for a while.

Clouds had started to gather overhead, and the change in weather seemed to reflect his change in mood. Suddenly, he wasn't so glad to be out again. Even though now he was free to come and go as he pleased, he felt more alone than ever.

How can I go home and tell them that I feel this way? he thought. *They'll think I'm nuts.* He considered turning around and heading back to the bar to clear his head. It had started to rain, and he wanted a place to get inside and sit down for a while. The rain began to fall harder as thunder rolled. Businessmen holding newspapers over their heads scrambled for their cars. Women in high heels skipped over the puddles beginning to gather on the ground, trying to carefully carry their purses and hold their umbrellas overhead without falling down.

The rain began to feel colder, and he decided he had better find a place to get inside. He turned the corner and saw St. Patrick's Church up ahead. He decided that would be an easy place to get out of the rain where nobody would bug him. He picked up the pace of his steps and quickly climbed the cement steps to the large wooden doors. He pulled open the heavy door and stepped inside. The door closed behind him, and the sound echoed throughout the empty church.

Here is a place that seems to be frozen in time, he thought. The old church was very familiar to Dominic. He had served Mass there countless times while he was growing up. He'd felt proud serving Mass in front of the entire congregation. But walking inside today, he felt terribly ashamed.

He was brought up in a good Christian home, raised Catholic by parents who loved God, and so did he. But somewhere along the line, he quit going to Sunday service. It wasn't that he had quit believing in God; he was sure He was out there. He just somehow had lost touch with Him. He wasn't sure how this had happened, but being there now, he felt ashamed that he had ever left.

He took a seat in one of the wooden pews. The wood creaked as he sat down. He glanced down at his watch: three o'clock. He planned just to sit there until the rain subsided; then he would be on his way home.

He looked around at the statues, which seemed to stare back at him, almost as if they expected him to do something. A statue of Mary, the mother of Christ, stood to the left of the main altar. The look on her face was comforting; it was almost telling Dominic, "Welcome back. It's very nice to see you again." Her outstretched arms seemed to convey the same idea.

On the opposite side of the church, in front of the right-side set of pews, stood a statue of Joseph, the father of Jesus. The statue held a carpenter's square in his left hand, and his right hand reached out to the people of the church. His face was sadder than that of his wife's; his look was that of empathy for those who looked upon him.

At the center of the church, behind the altar, a statue of Christ was suspended on the wall. Christ held out His arms in the same fashion His earthly parents were doing, welcoming the entire congregation. The ceiling in the church was very high and was adorned with scenes depicting the life of its namesake, St. Patrick. Large marble pillars separated the main part of the church from small sanctuaries dedicated to various saints of the church on both sides. Dominic recognized the faces of St. Jude and St. Anthony as he took a tour of the large church from his seat. They too seemed to encourage Dominic to do something.

He began to feel a little uneasy. Something inside told him that he should probably try praying as long as he was already there. He pulled out the kneeler and sank to his knees. No words came to mind. He felt guilty to ask God for anything, and he didn't feel like he had anything to be thankful for, so what was he going to say?

Dominic began to say the Lord's Prayer but quickly lost concentration. He began to think about all he had lost and became frustrated. His frustration caused him to sit back down in the pew as he kicked up the kneeler. "Forget it. What's the use anyway?" he said and then sat there in silence for some time, just waiting out the storm. How he would explain his tardiness to his family when he got home worried him. *Where am I going to tell them I was?*

The sound of the door opening and closing behind him at the back of the church interrupted his thoughts. The footsteps he heard approaching him in the main aisle made his heartbeat speed up a bit. He didn't turn his head to see who it was for the fear they would recognize him.

The footsteps drew closer, and he could hear their pace slow as they neared him. Dominic turned his head down and away, hoping to avoid any chance of confrontation. The footsteps now stopped, and he heard a man call to him with a strong but gentle voice. "Dominic?" He said nothing and didn't move. Although the voice had a familiar kindness to it, he didn't recognize it.

"Dominic, is that you?" This time, Dominic felt compelled to answer.

"Yeah, it's me," Dominic said, turning to face the man.

Chapter Two

The man had an old and kindly face, outlined by slight wrinkles. He had a neatly trimmed white beard, which matched the hair on his head. He was dressed in black and had a white collar on. He had his sleeves rolled up and carried a pencil and t-square in his right hand. The hairs on his forearms had a dusting of sawdust on them.

"May I sit down?" the old man asked.

"If ya want," Dominic said. They sat together in silence for a bit. Dominic wasn't quite sure what to say, and his manners were a bit out of practice, so he opted to ask the obvious. "I take it you're the priest here?"

"No, not here. Just came to do some work. Can't beat free labor, you know. Besides, I like working with my hands; it's almost therapeutic for me, you could say."

"I see."

"I help out at different churches as much as I can here and there. Guess I kinda just show up when my services are needed," he said as he held up his t-square.

"I don't get it," Dominic said. "So are you a priest or aren't you? I mean, the only people I've ever seen wearing a shirt with a collar like that are priests."

"Yeah, I am a priest," the old man replied. "Just so happens I have some work experience in other areas."

"Oh, I get it, I think," Dominic said. "But then how did you know me?"

"I've known your family for years. I'm sure you wouldn't recognize me. Last time I saw you, you were still pretty young."

"Sorry, I've been away for a while. I haven't really seen anybody in a long time."

"I know."

Who does this guy think he is? Dominic thought. *He seems to think he knows as much about my situation as I do. I thought I left these know-it-all personalities back in prison. I wonder what this guy wants from me.* "Oh yeah? What do you know about me?"

"Oh, I know more than you think," the old man replied calmly as he reclined back in the pew. "Your mother and I have gotten quite close since you went away."

"You're friends with my mom?" Dominic asked.

"Oh yes. Like I said, we've gotten quite close while you've been gone."

"What brought you and my mom to become friends?" Dominic asked. Dominic knew his mom consulted priests from time to time. She was a very religious woman, and it would not be unusual for her to befriend a priest. Still, this man's calm and almost happy demeanor made Dominic question his motive for sitting and talking with him.

"You know, you ask a lot of questions," the old man replied with a deep chuckle.

"Well, I don't recognize your face from anywhere, and I'm

not used to trusting people the past few years. I don't even know your name. You can't really blame me for questioning you."

"The name is Salvador, but you can call me Sal," the old man said, reaching out to shake Dominic's hand, which Dominic took hesitantly. "And as far as your mom and I being friends, she came to talk with me about you, and I was happy to listen. Anyway, you should know she thinks of you often. You're never too far from her mind."

"Yeah right. Out of sight, out of mind," Dominic said angrily. It wasn't that Dominic was angry with his family in any way. In fact, they were so supportive he didn't know where he would be without them. But being apart for so long, along with the changes in Dominic's character, put a definite strain on their relationship.

"You shouldn't be so tough on your mom; she's taken your situation very hard," the man said. "We've spent a lot of nights crying for you together."

"Really?" Dominic said as his voice broke. The thought of his mom crying made tears well up in his own eyes. He never meant to cause his mother pain. The very thought of the pain he had caused her made him hurt inside. "What about Dad? Are you friends with him too?"

"Yeah, I am."

"How's he doing?"

"He doesn't say as much as your mom," the old man said. "He tries to stay busy to keep his mind off of things, but I can assure you that you're never far from his mind either."

"Yeah?" Dominic said as a tear began to roll down his cheek. "What about the others?"

"Your sisters are doing just fine. They miss you and think about you all the time. You should know the whole family has taken your absence hard. Your pain was their pain, Dominic."

"I never meant to hurt any of them," Dominic said mid-weep. The single tear had become an uncontrollable weeping as he spoke. "I've missed them so much. I just don't know how I can make things right with them. I've missed so much while I was gone."

"I know," the old man said, now becoming a little choked up himself as he placed a hand on Dominic's shoulder. "They're not mad at you, Dominic; they know you didn't mean for all those things to happen. They love you, and they've missed you just as much as you've missed them. Even though you can be quite the handful at times, they still love you just as much as they always did." A grin now broke through the tears on his face.

"Yeah, I guess I can be, can't I?" Dominic said as a chuckle broke through the weeping. "You know, you're really good at making a guy feel better. How'd you get so good at that?"

"It's kinda what I do," the old man said as a smile ran across his face. "I listen and give counsel and comfort, and I help when I can."

"Oh yeah? You got work experience in the therapy field too?" Dominic asked.

"Some people might call it that," he said with a grin. "I've taken on all kinds of job titles over the years."

"Well, what should I call you?" Dominic asked.

"How 'bout just *friend* for now?" the old man said. "Wanna take a walk around this place?"

"Sure, friend," Dominic said with a smile. They stood up, and the man gave Dominic a gentle slap on the back as they moved to the center aisle. They walked down the aisle toward the front of the big, empty church. He didn't know if it was the man's kind face, his deep, soothing voice, or his strong hand on his back, but the man gave Dominic a sense of comfort he hadn't felt in a long time.

"So how have you been, Dominic?" the old man asked.

"I've been all right. Kinda lonely, I guess."

"Tell me more. It's been so long since we've talked."

"I'm sorry, but I can't ever remember talking to you."

"Well, it's been quite a while, but no time like the present for old friends to catch up."

"You and me were friends?" Dominic asked. The old man had caught him a bit off guard. He couldn't remember this man from anywhere, and now he claimed that they had been friends.

"I'd like to think so," the old man said with a smile.

"Well, like I said before, I've just been so lonely," Dominic said. "But I am starting to feel better, talking to you. I've just lost so much in the past eight years and in the years leading up to that night."

"Yeah, I know, but it's time to move on and forgive yourself for the past, Dom."

"But I've made so many mistakes. And some of those mistakes can never be taken back or made right again."

"No, that's true, but they can be forgiven," the old man said gently.

"Oh yeah? What would you know about forgiveness?" Dominic shouted. "You don't know me! You could never understand the pain I've gone through. Don't tell me about forgiveness. You could never help me with that." *This guy thinks he knows everything*, Dominic thought. *Was he there all those nights I spent in a cell crying over what I did? He could never understand how bad it hurts to deal with what happened every single day.*

"Oh, come on, what do you say we give it a try? Maybe, just maybe, I can help you find forgiveness," the old man said. "I think you and I have a little more in common than you think. Just please give me a chance to show you how much I care."

"Really, and just how do you intend to do that?" Dominic asked condescendingly.

"Come, take a walk with me," the old man said, holding out his arm.

Dominic moved next to him again, and they continued on their walk together. As they walked, Dominic caught a look at his hands. They were large and calloused. His skin, which had once been tan, was now wrinkled and faded. Walking with him in the silence of the church, Dominic once again felt at ease. He wasn't quite sure what they were walking to in that church, but Dominic was content just getting to know his newfound friend for the moment.

Chapter Three

The two walked side by side to the front of the big church. They sat next to each other in the front pew. From here Dominic could see the words "Come to me all you who are weary and I will give you rest" that were carved into the front lip of the marble altar. *Rest*, Dominic thought. *If there is one thing I could use, it's rest.* The statue of Jesus at the front of the church was now larger than life, and from here, Dominic could see His eyes, eyes that spoke more words of comfort and peace than any preacher Dominic had heard speak.

Even though the setting was peaceful, Dominic was having a hard time relaxing. Apparently the old man felt right at home because he immediately reclined back and crossed his legs. He turned to Dominic and asked, "So what's been going on since you came to see me last?"

"I told you, I don't have any idea where I've seen you before," Dominic said. *Why does this guy keep on insisting that we know each other? What does he want from me?*

"Well, let's see. The last time we talked, I remember you telling me that you were in school," the old man said.

"Yeah, well, that didn't work out so great for me."

"No? How come?"

"I just didn't really know what I wanted to do with my life, I guess," Dominic said. "Me and school books never really got along, you know what I mean?" The truth was that Dominic was always more concerned with partying than he ever was with school, a fact that Dominic was very aware of and only added to the list of regrets and what-ifs in his past.

"Yeah, I'm kind of a hands-on guy myself," the old man said.

"Yeah, I noticed your hands are pretty beat up. What did you do for a living?"

"Well, a little of everything, I guess you could say. I worked in construction for a while."

"Oh yeah? Where did you work?"

"My dad owned a small construction company. I kinda just fell into the family business."

"Yeah, that's kinda what I figured I'd always do too," said Dominic. "I mean, my dad owns his own business, as you know, and I guess I figured I'd end up taking it over someday. But now I have no idea what I'm going to do. I feel so lost." Working at his dad's steel mill never really made Dominic happy. He had grown up working for his dad and watched him develop a small company into a thriving business. And while Dominic always assumed his future had been decided for him since he was born, he always felt like there was more he could do. He just never figured out what.

"Well, I changed jobs when I was close to your age," the old man said.

"Really? What did you do?" *Maybe this guy could help me*

figure out where I can go from here. I'm so confused and lost right now; I'm open to suggestions.

"Well, I became a teacher. I got a job teaching a bunch of roughneck guys," the old man said. "They were kinda like you, all felt a little lost until I happened to run into them. Kinda like you and I happened to run into each other here today."

"What did you teach?"

"Oh, we covered all kinds of topics. I taught about life and love and the keys to happiness."

"I could really use some of that," Dominic said. He paused for a second. He looked at the floor and around the walls of the old church, wondering if he should ask his new friend to teach him what he had taught those men. He decided he had nothing to lose at that point. After all, he had been lost for so long he figured he'd at least listen to what the old man had to say. So he turned to him and asked, "Do you think you could teach me some of that stuff?"

"I was really hoping you'd ask that," the old man said with a smile, "but let's start with what you've been through already. After all, you don't know where you're going until you know where you're at. Okay?"

"Sure," Dominic said. "I'll see if I can answer the questions you have. I've got nothing to lose." Dominic hoped Sal wouldn't ask too many questions about his past. Dominic hated thinking about the accident. It was as if every time it was brought up, he had to live that horrifying experience all over again. It was bad enough to have to deal with the night terrors that still plagued him, so he avoided talking about it whenever possible.

"Fair enough," the old man said as a smile lit up his face. "Let's get up and walk around a little more; my old legs tend to get stiff if I don't keep them moving."

"Okay," Dominic said as the two stood up together. They continued their walk around the church. Dominic looked around the dark church, looking at the statues he hadn't taken much notice of as a boy. He was sure he knew more about them when he was younger, but now the faces and scenes of the statues and pictures that lined the walls of the church didn't mean much to him.

Dominic's attention turned to the man walking beside him. He noticed the old man looking around the room with a smile on his face. Almost as if he had been reading Dominic's thoughts, he turned to Dominic and asked, "What do you know about the people in these pictures?"

Dominic was kind of taken by surprise by the question. "Not too much," Dominic said honestly. "I mean, I know who Jesus is and all that, but I guess I never thought I had much in common with Him."

"Why is that?"

"Well...I mean, come on, what could I possibly have in common with the man who came to die for the world? Besides, I don't really think he had someone like me in mind when he was hanging on that cross," Dominic added as he pointed toward the cross that hung at the front of the church with a statue of Jesus's body attached to it.

"I think you have more in common with Him than you

think," said the old man. "And I think you're just the kind of guy he had in mind while he hung on that cross."

"Yeah right. If he knew he was dying for people like me who keep messing up things for themselves and the people around them, I don't think he would have gone through the trouble." *At least I wouldn't have gone through the trouble.*

"What do you mean by messing things up?" A look of concern fell over Sal's face.

"I've caused so much pain to the people I love. I've betrayed and let down those closest to me with my careless actions. I always thought about myself, never about how what I did affected them."

"Jesus knew what it was like to feel betrayed, but it never stopped Him from loving those who did it. I'm sure the ones you love feel the same way."

"Well, I don't know about that. All I know is that I've lost everything I love because I put myself before them."

"Well, it's true that you should always think of others before yourself," the old man said, "but what have you lost that means so much to you?"

"I've lost my best friend, the woman I love, time with my family because I was in prison, and to top it all off, I'm broke," Dominic said. The feelings of regret were now starting to overwhelm Dominic.

"Wow, you sound like a country song." The old man laughed.

"Thanks a lot," Dominic said. He knew exactly how pathetic he sounded. He didn't need this stranger rubbing it in his face.

"Oh, come on, cheer up," the old man said. "Money isn't everything, and you may find your love again; she's been there for you in tough times before. Your friend is in a better place, and I'm sure he forgives you for what happened. And your family is still here and loves and supports you. See, not everything is so bad."

"Yeah, I guess so," Dominic said. He had heard so many people say these words in an attempt to comfort him that now they had no comforting effect left in them.

"Now, getting back to you and Jesus," the old man said, "can you think of anything that you and He might have in common?"

What could I possibly have in common with someone as selfless as Jesus? I've spent my whole life doing what I thought would make me happy without any concern for anyone. "Not really. Don't think I've got much to relate to someone that was perfect," Dominic said. "I'm the furthest thing from that."

"Well, let's just see about that," said the old man. Their walk came to a stop in front of a picture hanging on the wall. The old man looked up at the picture. Dominic glanced at it but didn't pay much attention to it. He was anxious to hear what the man had to teach him.

The old man turned from the picture and looked over at Dominic, who had now become antsy and wandered away a bit. "Come back," the old man said. Dominic walked back over by the old man, who was still standing in front of the picture.

"Yeah? What's up?"

"Do you possibly have anything in common with this?"

the old man asked, pointing at the picture. Dominic looked up at the picture of Jesus, who seemed to be standing before a judge in the scene pictured. There was a small plaque underneath the picture that read, "Jesus is sentenced to death."

Chapter Four

The word *sentenced* jumped out at Dominic. This was something he understood all too well. He recalled standing in front of the judge the day he'd been sentenced. Just reading the plaque brought back the nervousness that had overwhelmed him then. He became uneasy. He read the plaque again. "Jesus is sentenced to death."

Recalling that day in the courtroom and hearing the judge deliver his sentence, he remembered it sure had felt like he was being sentenced to death. Though he wasn't literally being sentenced to death, at that time he figured he might just as well have been.

His future was being taken away from him. After all, isn't that really what death is? The lack of a future? When the judge had read that he would be in prison for eight years, he felt like they were throwing him in a hole to die. From the moment that sentence was read, he felt as though his life was over. Being in prison, what kind of a life was that? No jobs, no money, no nothing. People telling you where to be, what to eat, when to sleep, when to do everything. He remembered how his life had seemed to flash before his eyes. That would all be gone now.

He recalled his feelings from that day. He was a mess of

emotions. He had been overcome with sadness at what he was about to lose, and he was enraged that this had happened. It wasn't fair, he thought. He had already lost his best friend; now he was losing his family and his future.

Most of all, he'd been scared. Questions raced through his mind. What would happen to him now? Would he be forgotten? Would his family abandon him? He didn't know. He feared he would be on his own from that moment forward. He was so distraught at the possibility of the answers to the questions that he couldn't even say anything to his family before he left. He didn't hug them good-bye or cry into his mother's arms. He just stood there in a comatose-like state.

The feelings of that day began to overwhelm him again now. He looked at the ground, and in almost a whisper, he said, "Yeah, I sure can relate to that." Dominic walked over and sat in a pew. The old man came over and sat next to him.

"I thought you might be able to relate to that," the old man said.

A lump began to form in Dominic's throat. He didn't know what to say. He wondered where the old man was headed with this. He knew what he had been through, so why was he asking him this? He was supposed to be teaching him, not tormenting him.

The old man finally broke the silence and asked, "So do you think you know how Jesus felt when that happened to him?"

"He probably felt all the things that I felt the day of my sentencing."

"Tell me."

"Well, I felt mad, sad, and really scared all at the same

time, and I was only sentenced to eight years. I can only imagine that he felt all those things ten times more than I did."

"Yeah, I bet he did feel all those things," the old man said quietly.

"Yeah, well, at least His story has the upside of a happy ending. My story doesn't have such a happy ending."

"Your life isn't over, Dominic. The end of your story isn't written yet. And if you learn to follow and trust in God, you have a really good chance of writing yourself a happy ending."

Dominic began to recall the times he had spent with his friend all those years right up to the night of the accident. Smiles and laughter filled every memory he could recall other than the accident. The sights and sounds of that night began to creep into the back of Dominic's mind.

It was pitch black and cold. Dominic scrambled around the car. *Where was Eddy?* "Eddy!" Dominic screamed. "Eddy, where are you?" There was the faint sound of his friend's voice, but where was it coming from? Dominic began to panic. He could barely see his hand in front of his face; how was he going to find his friend?

"Dominic," he heard a voice call to him.

"Keep talking, Eddy," Dominic replied. "I'm going to find you."

"Dominic, are you okay?" This time Sal's voice snapped Dominic out of the momentary trance he had slipped into.

"Yeah, I'm fine," Dominic replied, trying to act calmly. "Just give me a second, okay?"

The thought of that night took a lot out of Dominic. He began to feel weak and tired.

Chapter Five

The two sat the end of a pew not too far away from another picture. The old man looked toward the picture on the wall. Dominic could see the scene depicted. Two men dressed as soldiers were handing a beaten Jesus the cross He would have to carry. The old man walked over and read the plaque underneath the picture they now stood before. "Jesus is given His cross." Dominic sat silent, expecting the old man to say something, but the old man just remained silent, gazing at the picture.

Dominic began to ponder how Jesus must have felt as he was given this cross to carry. He must have been so scared, especially knowing the task ahead of Him. He was to carry this cross only to be nailed to it when the journey was through. *How terrible, how utterly unfair,* Dominic thought. He had come to redeem the world, and this was the thanks He got. *Unbelievable. What a bunch of ungrateful people. Jesus would have given anything to save these people, and they put Him to death. What didn't they understand?* Anger began to build up inside of Dominic. He felt so mad at the people handing Jesus His cross. He had to say something. "How unfair," was the best he could come up with without completely exploding.

"Yeah, I was just thinking the same thing myself," the old man said. "But it was what His Father sent Him here to do."

"Yeah, but He didn't do anything wrong. He only wanted to help these people, and look at how they thanked Him," Dominic said sternly.

"They didn't know what they were doing," the old man replied calmly.

"How can you be so calm?" Dominic said, almost shouting now as he got up and walked toward the old man. "Doesn't this make you angry? I'll tell you one thing; I'm steaming mad just thinking about this."

"Are you mad for Jesus, Dominic? Or does this just remind you of what you went through?"

"Yeah, it makes me mad, but I did something wrong. I was at fault; don't you understand? I had a reason to be punished; He didn't."

"Yes, that is true," the old man said. "You made a mistake. Everyone makes mistakes, Dominic."

"He didn't," Dominic said, pointing to the picture in frustration.

"Well now, that isn't a very fair comparison, do you think?"

"Well, I guess not, but it still doesn't change what happened that night. If I had been thinking straight that night, the accident would have never happened."

"That's just it, Dominic," the old man said. "It was an accident. You never meant for that to happen; I know it, and everyone that you care about does too. You would have never hurt your friend intentionally. You did so much to help him while he was here with you, Dominic. The way you treated him, I'm sure it made God proud to call you one of His own."

The words touched Dominic somewhere deep down inside. They touched a place Dominic hadn't felt in a long time. He loved his friend as if he were his own brother, maybe even more so, and for someone to realize that caused Dominic to choke up. "Thanks," Dominic said in a whisper that was barely audible, tears welling up in his eyes.

"The day you were given your cross, Jesus wept for you along with all your family," the old man said.

"What cross?"

"The pain you went through as a result of that accident was a cross to carry. Jesus saw how heavy that cross weighed on you. He sees everything. He knows everything."

"How could He know how I felt?" Dominic blurted out through the anger as a tear rolled down the side of his face.

"He was there with you that night, watching over you," the old man said. "He saw how you cried in that jail cell. He saw how the pain of what had happened brought you to your knees that endless night. He was there; He cried every tear with you."

Sal put his arm around Dominic and pulled him close as tears fell like rain from Dominic's eyes. The pain of that night came back to him as if he was there experiencing it for the first time. He became angry at that pain. Why had Jesus let him feel so much pain? Why, if He loved him and shared his tears and his pain with him, did He let that happen to him?

These thoughts caused Dominic to push the old man away. "Why did God let that happen to me? If He was there with me, why didn't He take the pain away? Why didn't He just take me out of that awful place? You say that He loves me. How could He just sit on His throne up there and watch as someone you claim that He loves goes through so much pain?"

"It was a cross you had to bear, Dominic," the old man said calmly.

"That's it? That's all you have to say? That's the most wisdom-filled answer you can come up with?" Dominic asked coldly.

"We all have crosses to carry, Dominic," the old man explained. "While the cross you had to carry was a large and very heavy cross, know that God never gives anyone a cross that they cannot bear."

"Then why such a heavy load?"

"That load is what got you here today," the old man said. "It's going to allow God to form you into the person He wants you to be. That load has brought you and Him closer together. God gives the biggest crosses to the ones He wants to be closer to and whom He can trust to carry it well. That cross will allow you to experience God in ways many people never get to experience Him, but if you don't listen to His words and become a better man than you were before, then that opportunity is lost."

Dominic knew that what Sal was saying was true. He wanted to have what the old priest was talking about, but how? "What should I do?" asked Dominic. "I don't want to carry this load with me anymore. It's like I experience that night every night when I close my eyes. And it's the first thing I think about every morning when I wake up."

"Some crosses we have to carry for our entire lives," the

old man said. "I'm not promising that the pain from the loss of your friend will ever go away, but God can help you to drop some of the excess weight if you let Him."

Words of relief sounded like beautiful music to Dominic. Anything he could do to relieve some of this pain, Dominic would do. "I will do whatever He would want me to do," Dominic said. "Just show me the way."

"That's exactly what I plan on doing," the old man said. He threw his arm around Dominic and said, "Come, let's continue on our journey together."

Chapter Six

The two continued to walk in and out of the shadows of the pillars of the church. Dominic sniffled now and again, as his nose still ran from the crying he had been doing. Their walk led them in front of a bench made out of stone. Dominic sat on the bench and began to pour his emotions out to the kindly old priest.

"You know, the thought of what happened that night still causes me a lot of pain," Dominic said, looking at the ground. "It doesn't matter if I think about it in the morning or before I go to bed at night; it takes a lot out of me." He looked over at the old man.

"We all get tired, Dominic. This life throws a lot at us. Sometimes it seems to be a bit too much. Just remember what I said; our Father never gives anyone a load to carry that He knows they can't handle."

"I remember what you said, but it doesn't stop me from feeling overwhelmed sometimes. I don't know, maybe it's just me. Maybe I'm just too weak."

"It's okay to feel that way sometimes," the man said. "It doesn't make you less of a man or a weakling; it makes you human. Sometimes things get really tough, and we fall under the weight of our worries. Trust me; it happens to the very best of us."

The old man walked over to the picture on the wall in front of them. He looked at the picture, which was lit up by a small spotlight. Dominic watched as the priest ran his hand across the picture and lowered his head. "Yeah, sometimes things really get tough, but it's when things get tough you find out who you are inside," the old man said, looking back at Dominic.

Dominic rose to his feet and walked over to join him in front of the next picture. Dominic read the caption on the plaque underneath the picture. "Jesus falls the first time."

Dominic really had a hard time understanding this line. How could Jesus fall? He was God, perfect; how could he fall under the weight of the cross?

"Jesus fell?" Dominic asked the old priest, looking to him with a look of bewilderment on his face.

"Like I said, even the best fall down sometimes."

"But He was God. How could He become weak? I don't understand."

"Jesus is true God and true man," the old man said, "not just God. He felt all the same things you feel, Dominic. He knows what it's like to get tired and to feel weak. He knows what it's like to feel like you just cannot carry on anymore."

"But it's hard for me to keep going when I feel like that," Dominic said. "How do I get past those times?"

"Turn to Him in times of trouble, just like Jesus turned to His Father during times of trial in His life."

The words confused Dominic. How was he supposed to find God? "But where do I find Him?" Dominic asked. "I've gone through so many tough times in my life, and I've never seen Him before."

"Did you ever really look for Him, Dominic?"

How can I look for somebody that I can't even see? Dominic thought. *What is Sal talking about?* "Why do I have to look for Him? He's God; He's always here."

"That's true," the old man replied. "But if you don't turn to look for Him, how are you ever going to know how to find Him?"

"What do you mean?" Dominic couldn't understand. "I don't understand how to find Him."

"Well, He's not going to just show up in front of you," the old priest said, laughing. "Sometimes you have to search out for the answer you are looking for, and He is the answer, Dominic."

"So you're telling me if I turn to Him when I don't know what to do, He's going to fix things for me? He will pick me up when I fall?" *Sounds good to me. That is, if what Sal is saying is true.*

The old man chuckled. "Well, He's not going to come down and write the answer on the wall for you or reach down from heaven every time you fall. But if you seek Him, you will find Him. He won't give you the answer, but He will show you where to find it. He won't reach down from heaven to pick you up, but He will give you the strength to pick yourself up."

"Always?" Dominic asked.

"Always."

Dominic began to realize that he had been missing out on

something pretty special. He couldn't help but think that if he had known this before, things might be different. "Wish I would have realized this before," Dominic said. "Things probably would have gone a lot better for me up to this point."

"Hang on there, Dominic," the old man said. "This doesn't mean I can promise you a happy ending to every one of your problems." Sal raised his hand to Dominic to try to slow down his thoughts.

"You just said that God would help me get through the tough times if I—"

"I said that He would show you how to get through the tough times and give you the strength to get through the tough times," the old man said. "I never promised the outcome would be as you wish."

"Okay, I think I understand," Dominic said. "I wish it was how I said it though; things would be a lot easier." Dominic began to realize that a relationship with God didn't mean a free pass from life.

The old man laughed. "We tend to want everything given to us on a silver platter. Don't you think the guys upstairs ever get sick and tired of hearing us humans complaining all the time?"

"Thought you said they were there to listen and to help? Didn't realize they only did this as a part-time gig," Dominic said jokingly.

"Man, you're a fast learner." The old man chuckled. "You'd be a lot easier to pick on if you weren't listening so closely."

"Hey, you're the one who told me I had to listen," Dominic said.

The two stood in the shadows laughing together. *This is nice*, Dominic thought. *I haven't laughed like this in a long time.* He looked back over at the picture they stood in front of. He saw sweat and blood running down Jesus's face as he lay collapsed underneath the cross. "How do you think He felt then?" Dominic asked.

"Tired." The old man paused and sighed. "Alone too. He was in the middle of a big crowd at the time, but it probably felt like He was carrying that thing across an open field out in the middle of nowhere. You know what I mean?"

"Yeah, I do know what you mean. I've felt alone so many times. Even when I was around a lot of people, I never seemed to be with people who could really understand me. I know people tried to be there for me and understand what I was going through, but they could never really fully under-stand my pain, you know? That's what makes being here with you so great; you really try to understand exactly where I am and what I've gone through. You really listen, and it feels re-ally good to talk to someone like that for once."

"I'm glad you feel that way, Dominic," the old man said. "I'm really glad we're having this chance to talk too."

"Well, tell me when you're going to be here again," Do-minic said. "I'll make sure I'm here. Wouldn't miss it for the world."

"I won't be able to always be here like today," the old man said, smiling.

"What? Then how am I supposed to be able to talk to you?"

"I don't need to sit with you all the time. Just have a talk with Jesus, Dominic. Take time out from the world and go to Him in prayer. There's no set day or time; He's always with you through His spirit. All you have to do is tell Him what is on your mind in a small prayer."

"And He'll listen?"

"Of course He will. You need to think of Him as a friend. Don't just talk to Him when things are going poorly; tell Him about the good experiences you have too. He wants to know what makes you happy as well as what makes you sad, just like you would do with any of your other friends, okay?"

"Okay, I understand," Dominic said. "You don't have to leave yet, do you? I like being here with you."

"No, our walk isn't over yet," the old man said. "Come on, let's keep going."

Chapter Seven

The two continued their walk down the side aisle of the church in and out of the shadows that were cast by the marble columns of the church. The tops of the pillars were adorned with the faces of gargoyles, reminding the people of the Enemy's presence. The floor was made of two different colors of marble. The center of the aisle was a white marble, and the outside was a crimson shade. Dominic contemplated if what the old man had said was just that easy. When he was down, could he really just turn to Jesus and feel better automatically? Like some kind of switch to turn the pain and darkness off? He was beginning to understand that Jesus really did love him, but He wasn't physically going to be here with him to talk to and walk with. The old man told Dominic that.

So would knowing that He would be up there listening be enough? Dominic wasn't so sure, but he didn't want to ask the old man for an alternative plan. He didn't want him to feel like Jesus wasn't good enough for Dominic.

It would be nice to know that there was someone to turn to down here, Dominic thought. *Someone to take comfort in on an earthly basis, so to speak. Maybe I'll ask him later when we get to know each other a little better.*

The old man slowed his walk once again; he turned to Dominic and asked, "So who do you turn to when times are tough?"

"You already told me to turn to Jesus," Dominic replied. "Did I miss something?"

"No, you didn't miss anything," the old man said with a chuckle. "You are absolutely right. You can go to Him with anything. I meant in an earthly sense. Who do you turn to when things are tough? I know that sometimes it's nice to have somebody around who's physically present to talk to, like we are."

"You know, I was just thinking the same thing," Dominic said.

"What, God isn't good enough for you?" A look of bewilderment came across Sal's face.

"No, no, I didn't mean that at all," Dominic said emphatically.

"Relax," the old man said. "I'm just giving you a hard time. Like I said, I know it's nice to have someone physically present to talk to sometimes. People who care about you are a wonderful thing. I've had some good friends in my life, but most seemed to run out on me when things got really tough for me."

"Really?" Dominic asked. "So who was there for you? Who cared enough to stick out the tough times?"

"I had a great mother," the old man said. "She always stuck by me. It pained her so much to see some of the things I've been through, but she was there every step of the way." He pointed to the next image portrayed on the wall. The plaque underneath read, "Jesus meets His mother."

"Jesus had a very loving mother," the old man said with a big smile on his face.

"Yeah, I've got a pretty great mom too," Dominic said. The truth was Dominic cared for his mother very much. They didn't always see eye to eye, but the mutual love between mother and son ran deep. Dominic knew there was not a thing in the world that his mother would not do for him or his sisters, and if Dominic could, he would take back every ounce of pain he had caused his mom over the years.

"See, I told you that you have a lot in common with Him, Dominic."

"You know, she never seems to give up on me no matter how tough times have gotten," Dominic said, his eyes beginning to well up with tears. "She has been there for me in some of my darkest times. She was there all through my trial, and she visited me every chance she had while I was in prison."

"You see? Isn't that great?" the old man said. "To know that someone loves you enough to never give up on you?"

"Yeah, it really is," Dominic said, a tear releasing from the corner of his eye.

"Your face is telling a different story. What's the matter?" the old man asked, putting his hand on Dom's shoulder.

"I've just let her down so many times. You know? I feel so bad for making her go through all of this with me." Dominic couldn't even count how many times he had told her he would change his lifestyle, then, would fall back into his old habits again. There were family gatherings he had missed because he had been out the night before and all the lies told to make excuses for why he had not shown up. The thought of past failures made Dominic feel sick.

"Don't be sorry for that. Any great mother would do that without complaint, just like your mom has."

"Yeah, but she would have never had to go through that with me if I wasn't so stupid."

"You are not stupid, Dominic," the old man said. "Your actions have been very thoughtless at times, and I can see that you are sorry for what you did, as you should be. But never let the regretful feelings that you have outweigh the thankfulness that you have for the people who love you."

He's right. If I had been thankful for the people I love before, this whole mess would have never happened. "Okay," Dominic said, nodding in agreement.

"It has been tough for the both of you, but hasn't it brought you closer together?"

"Yeah, it has done that. Maybe the best part of losing some of my freedoms before I went to prison was the time I got to spend with my mom. It gave us a chance to hang out and talk a lot more. Don't get me wrong, she can be a very overbearing person sometimes." *I miss those times*, Dominic thought. *There are few things that I would rather do right now than spend a day with my mom just running errands and hanging out. Why don't I realize what means most to me until it's gone?*

"Well, sometimes mothers ask things of us that we don't necessarily want to do," the old man said. "I know how that feels for sure, but they are our mothers, and we just have to suck it up and obey them sometimes."

"Well, I haven't been so good at that last part so much. If I had been, I wouldn't have been in the mess I got myself into."

"That's for sure. The important part is that you learn

from that. You know those ten rules God gave Moses in the desert?"

"Yeah," Dominic said, "the Ten Commandments."

"That's right," the old man said. "There is a reason for the one in there about honoring your mother and father. It's very important that you do that. You may not always agree with them, but you must obey and honor them. Besides, in most cases, they know what they are talking about simply because they have been around longer."

I've never been good at following rules or listening to my parents, and look where it got me. "I understand," Dominic said. "I'll work on that for sure. It feels kinda silly saying that now that I'm almost thirty years old."

"It doesn't matter how old you get, Dominic. Do you expect them to love you less now that you are older?"

"No, I guess not."

"Then I think you owe them the same respect you always have, if not more. There may come a time when they might need your help as they get older. It may become a struggle for them to take care of themselves. It's important that you try to help them any way you can. After all, they played a major part in you being here."

Guess I never really thought of my parents getting old. They've done so much for me. I owe them whatever help I can give them if they ever need it. "Yeah, that's true," Dominic said. "They have just done so much for me, especially my mom."

"Someday, hopefully, you will be able to return the favor and be there for her when she needs you," the old man said.

"I really hope to get that chance. I know I would never be

able to repay all that she has done for me, but I hope to be able to help her in some way."

"I'm sure you'll find some way to do that. As long as you keep that attitude, I have no doubt in my mind that you will."

They both turned to look at the scene portrayed on the wall. Jesus was being driven on by the Roman soldiers as his mother stood by, tears streaming down her face. A look of despair was on her face as she gazed upon her son, blood and sweat pouring down His face.

"Oh, Dominic, no." Dominic looked at his mom as she spoke these words of shock. He could see the tears about to fall from her eyes. The guard led him from the courtroom and away from his life. Dominic stared back at his mother, but no words came from his mouth. He could not believe what the judge had just said. Eight years. Life would never be the same. "You know, that reminds me of what happened right after I was sentenced as they hauled me off to prison," Dominic said. "That was such a tough day. I won't ever forget the look on my mom's face."

"Yeah, but isn't it great to have a mom that is willing to go through anything with you?"

"Yeah, it sure is."

"Mothers are a wonderful gift from God," the old man said. "Don't forget that, okay?"

"I won't," Dominic said with a smile.

"Good, now come on. Let's keep going; we still have a lot to cover," the old man said, slapping Dominic on the back.

Chapter Eight

D ominic was wondering how long the old man would talk with him. He didn't want him to leave. He was learning so much from him, but even more than that, he was happy there with him.

Dominic looked over at the old man. He had a good, solid build to him. His broad shoulders had now drooped a bit, but it was evident that he had been strong in his younger days. *Being a construction worker years ago must have been tough work,* Dominic thought. *Fewer power tools, more hand tools. That must have been some tough work.* Dominic figured anyone who worked in construction in that era would have had a strong build. He probably hauled a lot of lumber around by hand.

Dominic figured he was pretty lucky to be able to spend time with such a wise old priest. If he couldn't talk to God face-to-face, he was sure his newfound friend was the next best thing. Dominic had only known him for what seemed to be a couple of hours, and he had already learned so much from him.

Christina and Evan. Other than my family, they are the only ones who really listened to me the way Sal is listening to me. Has it really been eight years since I've seen them?

With the exception of Eddy, Christina and Evan were Dominic's closest friends for as long as he could remember. *Without their help, I don't think I could have dealt with losing Eddy*, Dominic thought. However, after he was sentenced, he had lost contact with Evan. And Christina, well, it just didn't work with Dominic being in prison.

In the corner of the church, Dominic saw a statue of Jesus carrying the cross. He wondered how anyone could endure what He had gone through, let alone without any help. He was able to handle it all by Himself. That was another thing about Jesus that Dominic could identify with, for sure. He didn't like asking for help either. He was kind of a one-man show. When it came to a task, he would just as soon do it by himself. *That's pretty cool*, Dominic thought. *Guess I am kind of like Him after all.*

The old man turned and leaned against a pillar of the church. He put his hands in his pockets and said, "You know, sometimes we just can't do it all by ourselves."

"You mean us humans," Dominic said.

"Yeah, I mean us humans," the old man said. "Jesus included."

"What are you talking about? He was God; He didn't need any help, ever."

"What are you talking about?" the old man replied. "Like it or not, He was also one hundred percent human, and His human body was about ready to call it quits at one point, and He needed a hand."

"A hand with what?"

"With carrying His cross."

"Let me get this straight," Dominic said. "Jesus, God made man, needed help carrying a couple of pieces of lumber?"

"That's what I'm telling you," the old man said with a laugh.

"Yeah, okay," Dominic said, "tell me another one. You had me going there for a minute. I get it, you have a sense of humor too. Never took you for a kidder." *He can't be serious. God doesn't need help.*

"I'm serious, Dominic," the old man said. "I'm not joking at all. Go check it out for yourself." He pointed over to yet another small lit spot on the wall.

Dominic walked over to the scene depicted there. A man was now standing next to Jesus in the scene. He had Jesus's cross on his shoulders. Jesus also leaned against the man heavily. The plaque underneath the scene read, "Simon helps Jesus carry the cross."

Dominic really couldn't believe what he was reading and looking at. He had always heard that Jesus had come to die for him and for everyone, but it finally hit him that he never really understood what all went into the purchase of salvation.

"You look pretty surprised, Dominic," the old man said.

"Well, I am. I guess I never really thought or knew how tough this whole thing was for Him."

"Yeah, it must have been an extremely tough thing to do. Just imagine; He was on His last legs at this point. He had already been beaten badly, and He really didn't have much strength left. He must have been more than happy to have a little help lugging that tree up that hill where He won your salvation."

"I guess I'm just surprised He actually needed help," Dominic said, "or even that He was willing to have help carrying the cross."

"We all need a little help sometimes," the old man said. "Sometimes it's physical, sometimes not. It can be a pretty humbling experience asking for or just allowing someone to help us sometimes. The thing that usually gets in the way is pride. Pride can be a very bad thing, and it can hurt us."

The truth was, after the accident, it took months for Dominic to open up to anyone, despite how much those who loved him said they would help any way they could. And once he had been locked up, it was the same story. He told them he was fine and just needed to be left alone. He didn't want anyone to think he couldn't handle what he was going through or for them to think he was weak. "I guess I am pretty prideful," Dominic said. "I don't really like asking for help much."

"Well, pride can be a good thing too," the old man said. "It's good to take pride in your beliefs, it's good to take pride in your work, and it's good to take pride in your family. But when you are in a position where you could really use some help, pride gets in the way. That's when a little humility goes a long way."

Dominic remembered the day he finally let Christina know how badly he was really hurting. It felt so good to finally let someone in. A couple days later, Evan had come over, and Dominic spilled his guts to him and cried like a baby. From then on, they were there right up until his day of sentencing. "Yeah, I guess you are right," Dominic said. "I had a couple of friends show up when I least expected them to when I was going through the toughest time in my life too."

"Didn't it feel good to know that someone was willing to help?"

"Yeah, it really did. I really wasn't expecting anyone to show up and offer their help to me. Especially after most of the people I considered my friends kinda disappeared after the accident." *Tommy, David, Joey, Jimmy, they were all out with us the night of the accident, and they all just disappeared after that.* Just thinking about them irritated Dominic. *How could they have done that to me? I was always there for them, but when I needed help, they all disappeared. I still can't believe they did that; it still hurts.*

"I hear you there," the old man said emphatically. "It hurts to lose friends who you thought would always be there no matter what; I know that. But it really makes you appreciate the friends and even sometimes the strangers who are willing to be there in time of need."

"Yeah, I hear you," Dominic said. "It was really awesome to have so many people show support for me through the whole trial process. I had someone who was kind of my Simon too, my buddy Evan. Kinda held me up when I was about ready to give up. I can't even remember how many nights we spent just hanging out, watching television or shooting pool. If I wanted to talk, he would listen, but he never forced the issue either."

"I'm so happy that he could be there for you," the old man said.

"Yeah, I really hope I can get in touch with him pretty soon, now that I'm out. I miss hanging out with him."

"You really find out who your friends are in times of crisis, don't you?"

"Yeah, you really do. Some just scatter. Hard to know if they were ever really your friends in the first place."

"Well, you're certainly right about that," the old man said, "but it's times like that when the cream rises to the top, so to speak."

"I guess it's better to find out the hard way than to never really know who your true friends are," Dominic said.

"I think so too," the old man said. "Another thing to think about when it comes to friends is that some people may care about you but just don't know how to handle a certain situation you may be in. Don't just write off a relationship because some good friends may scatter at times when they are scared or just confused about a situation."

"Yeah, I guess you've got a point there," Dominic replied. "But when you look around and nobody is there, it makes you kinda mad. Especially when those friends disappear who you've done so much for and would drop everything to help."

"I'm sure Jesus can understand you there," the old man said. "He came to save mankind, and His own disciples couldn't even stick it out with Him. I'm sure He was pretty disappointed in them at that time."

"Yeah, good and faithful friends are hard to come by."

"Sad but very true. Come on, we've got a few more things to talk about," he said, slapping Dominic on the back.

"Okay, but only if you promise not to hit me so hard again," Dominic said, joking. "I'm not so young anymore."

The old man smiled. "You know, Dominic, you're quite a handful, but I love you."

Dominic was kind of weirded out by this comment; after all, he had only known the man a few hours, and he was telling him that he loved him? But he didn't want to hurt the man's feelings; after all, he was just an old priest. He meant no harm by his words. "I love you too," Dominic said as he put his arm around the old man.

The carefree feeling Dominic felt with Sal was something of the past to Dominic. *When is the last time I felt like this?* Dominic wondered. *Before the accident? No, longer. Before Christina and I broke up. The lake.*

"Don't do it, Eddy," Dominic said as he floated backward in the water. "If you jump in from that high, there won't be any water left in the lake." Dominic could barely finish as he started to laugh.

"Ha ha, very funny, Dominic," Eddy said as he climbed up to the rocky ledge sticking out over the edge of the lake. "You know, words can hurt a guy, especially a sensitive guy like myself."

"Wait up," Evan called up to Eddy as he scrambled up to the ledge behind him. "Together we'll be able to blast him out of the water."

"You guys are crazy," Christina interjected. "If somebody listened to you guys talk, they'd think you hated each other."

"Hurry up, Evan," Eddy called down, "or he'll swim too far out to be able to drench him good."

"I'm coming, just settle down," Evan called back. "He can't swim that fast anyway."

"Aren't you even going to try to save me?" Dominic called out to Christina, who was still standing on the shore, as he held up his arms in seeming dismay.

"You got yourself into this mess," Christina joked back. "Now you have to suffer the consequences. Sorry, babe."

"Guess I see where I rank," Dominic joked back.

"Caaannnon baaalll!" Eddy and Evan screamed as they jumped from the ledge.

In an instant, water was rushing over Dominic like a tidal wave. His urge to laugh was so strong he almost forgot to take a breath as he went under the surface. "You guys really know how to make an entrance," Dominic joked as he broke through the surface of the water. "I see I was wrong."

"Wrong about what?" Eddy asked.

"There is still water in the lake," Dominic said with a big grin on his face.

"Get over here," Eddy said as he swam after Dominic.

"Help, Christina! Help!" Dominic cried playfully.

"If you guys weren't so much fun to be around, I might think about leaving," Christina yelled back as she jumped in.

Those were really good times, Dominic thought. *Man, I really miss those guys.*

Chapter Nine

Y ou know," Dominic said, "there aren't many people who are willing to lend a hand when times are tough."

"What do you mean?" the old man asked.

Dominic took a couple seconds to sort his thoughts. He ran his hand through his thick, black hair and scratched the back of his head. "I mean that there might be a lot of people out there who care or sympathize with the situation that you're in, but not that many are willing to get too close to the problem."

"That is true. What made you think of that?"

"I was just thinking about a girl I knew before I went to prison." Recalling the day at the lake made it hard for Dominic to get Christina out of his mind. All she had done for him and what she meant to him began to build up inside of him.

"What about her?" the old man asked.

"Well, I was thinking about how Simon helped Jesus carry the cross and how he kind of came out of nowhere to help Him, and I guess talking about people who want to help made me think of her."

The old man sat down with his hands between his knees

and leaned forward. "You are talking about Christina, aren't you?"

Is this guy a mind reader or something? "Yeah," Dominic said. "How did you know?"

The old man leaned back and opened his arms. "Come on, who are you talking to? We're friends. Besides, anyone could tell who you were talking about by that twinkle in your eyes."

"I guess I was always a sucker for that girl," Dominic said with a grin.

"What makes her so special to you, Dominic?"

"Well, like I said, I always was a sucker for her. But I guess the thing that really makes her special in my mind is that she showed up when I least expected her to."

"Why didn't you expect her to show up?"

"Well, our relationship before the accident wasn't exactly pleasant or even cordial, but she showed up and acted as if none of that was even an issue. She treated me with such kindness and care." As their relationship came to a close, a lot of arguments had taken place between Dominic and Christina. What had once been a relationship that showed promise for the future broke down, and they took it out on each other. It had ended one night in front of Dominic's house. Christina drove away and didn't look back. Dominic didn't blame Christina for giving up on them, but it did hurt, no doubt about that. So when she showed up, it took a while for Dominic to warm up to the idea of being around her again.

"And it's surprising to you that she could be nice?" the old man asked.

"No, I don't mean that," Dominic said, "but like I said before, all of my friends kind of scattered, and Christina and I weren't even friends anymore. Yet she showed up and acted as if we had been friends all along."

"What did she do that made her so exceptional in your mind, Dominic?"

"Man, you really ask a lot of questions sometimes," Dominic said with a chuckle.

"Well, I want to know what you're thinking," the old man said.

"Well, I guess what made her so special to me wasn't that she took so much of her time to come visit me or even all the nights she spent talking on the phone with me."

"Then what was it?"

"I guess it was more just the simple kindness and the love she showed me that meant the most," Dominic said. "I guess she acted just like you are acting now. She reminded me of what I think Jesus would be like."

"Wow," the old man said. "That is a huge compliment to give to someone."

"Yeah, I know, but it's true. I mean, she showed kindness to someone who wasn't even nice to her. She showed love when the latest memories of us had been ones of hate."

I don't know what I would have done without her, Dominic thought as he recalled a night a few months after the accident.

"I didn't mean for it to happen," Dominic said as his face became red and his eyes welled up with tears. "I just can't believe he's gone."

"I know you didn't," Christina said as she got up from her

chair and walked over next to Dominic on the couch. "Eddy knows you didn't mean for it to happen." Christina put her arm around Dominic.

"It was like one second we were joking and having fun, and the next second the world stopped turning." Dominic buried his face in his hands and began to weep.

"I know, I know," Christina said, pulling Dominic into her arms. "Come here. It's going to be okay." Words Dominic had heard so many times but never believed until they came from her lips.

That's when I started to heal, Dominic thought. "I could never repay her for that," Dominic said to Sal as he turned to face him.

"A gentle hand and some kind words can go a long way," the old man said. "Love doesn't have to be expressed through big, expensive gifts or a fancy dinner or a big ring. In fact, most times it's the smallest things that express the most love. You know, there was someone on Jesus's journey that showed Him that kind of love." The old man pointed over to the wall.

Dominic walked over to another scene depicted on the wall. There was a woman standing in front of Jesus. She was offering Him a towel to wipe His face. The plaque underneath the scene read, "Veronica wipes the face of Jesus."

Dominic smiled as he read the plaque. He thought of Christina again. With that same smile, he turned to the old man and said, "That's got Christina's name all over it."

"Do you think that she knows you feel that way?"

"I don't know. I've never been really good at telling people how much they mean to me, and I guess I never really realized how much she meant to me until I talked to you."

"Well, I am glad that I'm helping you see things a little differently, Dominic," the old man said. "But don't give me too much credit. I think it's because you are starting to see things through the eyes of Jesus and are becoming His friend. You know, when you allow yourself to become friends with Him, it's easier to begin to see Him in others."

"What do you mean by that?" Dominic asked.

"I mean that when you open up your heart to Jesus, you open up your heart to love. He is love, Dominic, and when you open your heart to Him, it's easier to see the good in others because you look at others through love."

"You know, I never thought of things this way before," Dominic said. "Wish we woulda had this talk a long time ago."

"Well, like I said, it's not so much what I have said today, it's that you're starting to find Jesus in your life. Why didn't you ever come look for Him before?" the old man asked.

"What do you mean?" Dominic asked. "I never knew where to look for Him, and I didn't look for Him this time. You helped me find Him."

"No, you found Him yourself. I just helped you open your heart to Him. He has always been here; you have just never taken the time to notice Him. Just like you never took the time to realize how much Christina meant to you."

"I really am sorry I didn't feel this way before," Dominic said. "I never realized I was neglecting God. I guess I just thought God was supposed to come to me; I never thought I had to find Him. I am so sorry I didn't start a better relationship with Him before."

"You're forgiven, Dominic," the old man said. "God doesn't hold grudges against those who love Him. Just do me one favor."

"You name it, you got it."

"Don't let the people that mean the most to you go by without you telling them how much they mean to you."

"You got it," Dominic said. "I promise to do a better job of doing that."

"Good," the old man said. "You need to hold yourself to that promise. Now let's keep moving; we don't have much farther to go."

Chapter Ten

Talking with this old, wise man really made Dominic think of all that Jesus had done for him. He came to die for him and the rest of the world, knowing that most of the time people would forget about Him. And to top it all off, the way He had died for the world was so terribly painful.

Dominic now began to wonder how Jesus had accomplished all this. He clearly was tired at this point on His journey of bringing salvation to the world. If He needed help just to be able to carry His cross, how did He make it to the crucifixion? Where did He find the strength to keep going? Of course Dominic understood that He was God, but the old man had said He was true God and true man. If that was true, Dominic couldn't understand how He could find the will to keep going, especially when the very people He came to bring salvation to were the same people doing this to Him. Even His closest friends had basically given up on Him at this point. They weren't even the ones who helped Him carry the cross; they had to get a complete stranger to help Him.

With all these things going on around Him, Dominic couldn't understand why He just didn't give up. Why didn't He just lay down and die right there? Wouldn't that get the job done? Wasn't it good enough that they would have killed the son of God? If all He had to do was come and die for man, why continue with this torture? Dominic didn't know, and all these questions began to trouble him.

He leaned against the wall. He noticed another scene on the wall next to him. Jesus was on the ground again. The plaque on the wall read, "Jesus falls a second time." Dominic sighed.

"Something on your mind?" the old man asked.

"Yeah, but I'm not really sure if I should ask or not."

"Go ahead, don't be scared. You can ask me anything."

"Promise not to take it the wrong way?" Dominic asked. "I mean, I don't want it to seem like I'm questioning God or anything."

"Of course I won't get mad, Dominic," the old man said. "And it's okay to question God; in the end, it will bring you closer. The answer to your questions will be answered by how much He loves you."

"Okay, well, I was just wondering..." Dominic paused.

"Yes?"

"Well, I was just wondering why Jesus didn't just give up if He was so tired? If He just had to come and die for us, wasn't this enough to do the job already?"

"No, it wasn't enough yet." A look of concern fell on the man's face.

"Well, why not? I mean, He is the Son of God, for goodness' sake; why all the torture? Couldn't He just decide that this was enough? Doesn't He make the rules, after all?"

"Yes, He does make the rules," the old man said with a chuckle. "But the job wasn't done yet. He had to keep going to prove to you and to the rest of the world just how far He was willing to go to save you. He had to show you how much He loves you. No price was too high to pay for you. He wasn't willing to give up on that message. Besides, He wasn't done with the job His father sent Him to do."

"Oh yeah," Dominic said, "that whole obedience thing, huh?"

"Yeah, that's right," the old man said with a smile. "But it was just as much to show you how much He loves you. There is no greater love than to lay one's life down for his friends."

These words took Dominic by surprise. He had heard of God's love, but never in such a personal way. "Who, me?"

"Yeah you," the old man said with a laugh. "Hard to believe, huh?"

"Well, yeah, especially because I wasn't even born yet."

"Oh, He knew you long before anyone down here knew you or you even knew yourself, and He loved you."

"Well, I'm flattered," Dominic said. "I just wish He didn't have to go through all this just for me."

"You were worth it to Him, and because He did, someday you will be able to spend the rest of eternity with Him."

"You mean someday I'll be able to be with Jesus the way you and I are together right now?"

"That's what I'm sayin'."

"I could get used to that," Dominic said.

"I'm sure He can't wait to see you up there," the old man said, looking up at the sky, "but you still have a long life ahead of you down here."

If God loves me this much, there must be something I can do to show Him that I love Him too. "Well, what can I do to make Him proud as long as I have to be here for a while longer?" Dominic asked.

"Just don't crucify Him anymore."

"*What?*" Dominic asked with shock. "I didn't crucify Jesus."
Just when I think I am starting to understand this whole thing, he goes and says something like that? You gotta be kidding.

"You may not have held the nail as He was hammered to the cross, but He came to pay for your sins, Dominic," the old man said. "Just try to lead a good life from now on is what I mean. Use the talents that God gave you for the good of others. Be His hands and feet while you're here on earth, and I promise you, someday you will be together with Him in all His glory."

"Well, how can I turn my back now, knowing all this?" Dominic asked. "I will try to do His work while I'm here, I promise."

"Glad to hear it," the old man said as he put his arm around Dominic. "Come on, we have a little more to go."

Chapter Eleven

Y ou know, there are a few more friends that Jesus met along His way to Calvary," the old man said. "You know, I'd be willing to bet the good He saw in some of the people He met along the way really reminded Him of the good in people, despite all the hate He was experiencing."

"I can't imagine how He could see any good through all of this," Dominic said. "This was such a horrible thing He went through. How could He ever see any good in it?"

"There is always some good that comes through, even in the worst times, Dominic," the old man said. "You just need to have faith that God will show you the good in the bad. Even the worst situations have the capability to bring about something beautiful and awe-inspiring. It can come through in all sorts of ways, but in His case, as in many, it came through in the people around Him."

He's sure right about that, Dominic thought. *All those cards people sent and all the phone calls from people were amazing.* "Well, now that you put it that way, I can definitely relate. When I went through my ordeal, the people of this town were really great to me and showed me a lot of support."

"You see, there is one more thing that you guys have in common. Some of the people in His town really came through for Him when He took His journey too, see?" The old man pointed to another scene depicted on the wall next to them.

The scene showed women holding out their hands toward Jesus. Many of them were crying, and all of them had a very sad look upon their faces. The plaque underneath the scene read, "Jesus meets the women of Jerusalem."

The scene depicted on the wall made Dominic think of the day he was sentenced. So many people from Riverdale had shown up to show their support for him. "Wow, I bet that was kind of neat for Him to see those people who loved Him and came to show their support and concern for Him," Dominic said.

"I'm sure it was."

"My situation was pretty similar to that. I got so many letters from people, and a lot of them even stopped over to see me and to visit me for a while."

"Makes things a little easier when you know that there are people out there who care about what you are going through, doesn't it?"

"Yeah, it really does. You know, none of them had to take time out of their days to come and see me, but they did. That really did mean a lot to me. I wish I could repay them in some way."

"Well, just do what Jesus did," the old man said.

"Whoa there," Dominic said. "You know I'm grateful, but I really don't feel like dying for them."

"No, not that, ya goofball," the old man said. "I just mean that you can show them how much they mean to you by what you do for others."

Again, what the kind priest said made Dominic think. *How can what I do for others repay the people who were kind to me?* "How does that work?" Dominic asked.

"Well, by doing good for others, you show those who helped you that you are passing on the love that they showed to you," the old man said. "All those people that showed support for you want the best for you, and you can show them that you appreciate what they did by putting their love to good use and pass it along to another."

"I get it. Kinda like that whole pay-it-forward thing."

"Yeah, just like that. Of course, a simple thank you or a letter goes a long way too."

"I guess I kind of took some of those people for granted," Dominic said.

"How so?"

"Well, I wasn't too good about saying thank you to those people, and I haven't been able to do much to help others being locked up for the past few years."

"You know, it is never too late to say those thank yous, and it certainly is never too late to do good for others."

This is the time to start changing my life. "You're right," Dominic said. "I'm not gonna waste any more time. I'm going to start living my life the way that I should have been all along. Stop being so selfish and think of others for a change."

"That is what I like to hear," the old man said.

"Well, you are a very good teacher," Dominic said. "You'd have to be to get through to a guy with such a hard head like me."

"Thanks, but don't forget, God is the one who gave you that hard head, so put it to good use."

"Uh, what do you mean?" Dominic asked. "Most people tell me to stop being hardheaded and stubborn, not to put it to good use."

"Well, I mean being stubborn can sometimes be a good thing."

"How so?"

"Well, it's a good thing to stand firm when it comes to your beliefs," the old man said. "And standing firm in your own beliefs can do a lot for others to confirm their beliefs."

"It's always about helping someone else with you, isn't it?" Dominic asked.

"It has to be. That's how you spread the love that God gave to you, by thinking of others first. Without love, we are nothing."

"Okay. I can understand that."

"There's just one more thing," the old man said.

"What's that?"

"You need to learn how to forgive the people who have done wrong to you."

"Well, like who do you mean?" Dominic asked.

"Well, you talked about some friends that had turned their backs on you when you were going through your whole ordeal."

"Yeah, what about them? I don't want to see those guys ever again," Dominic said with an angry tone. *If he expects me to forgive those guys, he can forget it. I was always there when they needed me, and when I needed them, where were they? Forget it. All of them knew exactly what happened, and they turned and ran the opposite direction. I haven't heard from them since that night. Forgive them? No way.*

"I'm not saying you have to go out and be best friends with them," the old man said, "but you do have to find it in your heart to forgive them."

"Forget it," Dominic said with a scowl. "I don't need to forgive them. I always did whatever I could for those guys, and they thanked me by running out on me."

"Haven't you ever turned your back on anyone?"

"No, absolutely not," Dominic said, almost yelling now. "I've tried to be a good friend always. I'd drop whatever I was doing to help any of my friends out."

"What about your mom and dad? Didn't you turn your back on the way they raised you? And what about God? Haven't you closed your heart to Him until now?"

That's not the same thing; don't even try to tell me that! Dominic wanted to snap back at Sal but fought back the urge. "Well, yeah, but my parents forgive me for what I put them through; I have apologized to them. And God knows I'm sorry for what happened and that I haven't spent more time with Him in prayer. I told you all that."

"Your parents forgave you unconditionally, just as many good parents forgive their children," the old man said. "But don't you want God to forgive you too?"

"You said that He forgives us and that He loves us and that is why He came to die for us. That's what you said, remember?"

"Oh yeah, I remember, but how can you expect God to

forgive you for all the things that you have done to hurt Him when you can't even forgive others yourself?"

Sal's words made Dominic stop and think. *He's right. If I can't forgive others, how can I expect God's forgiveness for myself?* "Yeah, well, when you put it that way, it's hard to argue with you," Dominic said.

"And?" the old man said questioningly.

"And," Dominic said hesitantly, "and I'll try to forgive them the best that I can. Maybe we can get together for a barbecue or something. I'm not willing to forget just yet, but I can start trying."

"That's all God wants. Don't forget, Jesus was human; He knows how hard it is to forgive others."

"All right, I'll try."

"Good," the old man said. "Come on, we've got some more to cover."

Chapter Twelve

The two were now walking toward the back of the church. On the back wall of the church was a portrait of Jesus. In front of the portrait stood a kneeler and a set of votive candles, some of which were lit and some that were not. The flag of the Catholic Church stood in the corner of the church, closer to the portrait of Christ, and mirroring it in the opposite rear corner of the church stood the flag of the United States. Dominic couldn't help but notice the feeling of comfort that the portrait of Christ radiated. The feeling was similar to that which he felt talking to Sal. If the goal was to become Christ-like, Dominic was sure Sal had reached that goal. He had never felt like this with anyone else. He was compassionate and loving. He took the time to understand Dominic, and in just a few hours, Dominic felt as if this man knew him better than anyone else, maybe even better than Dominic knew himself. He wasn't quite sure what it was about the old man that made him feel this way. *Well, chalk it up to life experience, that's how he knows so much*, Dominic thought.

Just then, the old man stumbled and fell to one knee. "Whoa there, you okay?" Dominic asked as he reached down a hand to help him up.

"Yeah, I'm okay. Just give me a minute to recuperate. Old bones, you know," he said with a chuckle.

"Yeah, sure, I'm in no hurry," Dominic said, dropping to one knee to join the man on the ground.

Dominic looked into the man's face. He felt like he should recognize him from somewhere. It was like he had been seeing that face and those eyes his entire life, but where had he seen them? Dominic turned away so that the man wouldn't notice that he was staring.

His gaze landed on a portrait of Jesus on the back wall of the church. The portrait of Jesus had the same kindly face and same dark eyes of the man he was talking to now. "Didn't notice that before," Dominic said out loud to himself.

"What's that?" the old man asked.

"Well, you really look a lot like that picture of Jesus over there. Kinda weird, huh?"

"Is it weird? Or are you just beginning to see who I really am?"

This guy isn't saying what I think he is, is he? "What do you mean by that?" Dominic questioned.

"Don't be afraid, Dominic," the old man said. "Let your eyes see what your heart knows to be true."

Dominic couldn't believe what he was hearing. He became angry. He stood up from the pew and stepped back, looking at the old man. He didn't know what to say. He knew he had been gone a long time, but what did this old man take him for, an idiot? This guy must be out of his mind; the years must have gotten to his head. How could this guy come and claim to be the Son of God? Who did he think he was, anyway?

Making a claim like that, this man was obviously insane. He was the one who should have been locked up, not Dominic. The thought of this made Dominic even angrier.

"What are you, some kind of a nut?" Dominic asked. "Who do you think you are, walking in here and claiming to be the Son of God?"

"Seems to me like I've heard that before," the old man said calmly. "You know, the people who had me on trial that day told me the very same thing you're saying now. I hope things turn out better between you and me than they did that day."

"What are you talking about?" Dominic asked angrily. "Everyone knows the story of Jesus; I could go up to someone and make the same claims you are, using that lousy reasoning. What you just said is common knowledge. You don't have to be Jesus to know those things."

"Why don't you believe, Dominic?"

"Because Jesus doesn't come down from heaven anymore. Not until the end of the world anyway. Is that what you're going to say next?" Dominic asked sarcastically. "That this is the end of the world?" The old man sat there without saying a word. "Got nothing to say now, huh? Bet you didn't count on me knowing that, did ya? The gig is up. I'm outta here." Dominic walked to the door.

"Look at your watch," the old man called after him.

Dominic looked at his watch; the digital numbers read 3:16, probably around the time the old man walked into the church. The seconds had quit counting. *Great*, Dominic thought, *stupid watch needs a new battery.*

"Yeah, so what? I have a junky old watch and it needs a

new battery. See ya later." *What a nut job*, Dominic thought as he walked toward the door.

"That's not very nice to say about someone," the old man called out.

Dominic stopped and looked back at him. *How did he hear that?* He must have said it out loud by accident. He felt kind of embarrassed.

"Sorry, didn't mean to say that out loud," Dominic apologized and continued to walk toward the door.

"You didn't," Dominic heard the old man say as he pulled open the door.

"Yeah, whatever you say." The words flew out automatically at the ridiculous statement as he looked back at the old man. He turned to look outside. He couldn't believe what he saw. The rain had frozen mid-fall in the sky. He walked to the bottom of the steps onto bare ground. There were no cars and no streets. No buildings, no people, no nothing. Just clear ground and sky. Dominic walked back up the steps and opened the door to the church. He slowly walked into the church. He saw the old man sitting there in the same place he had left him.

The old man turned around to look at Dominic and asked with a grin, "Back so soon?"

"Ha ha, very funny. What is this, some kind of a joke?"

"No no, no joke. You see, I thought you needed to take a timeout from life and really think about things."

"What do you mean?"

"You're dead, Dominic," the old man said, becoming serious.

"What!" Dominic said with a startle.

"Just kidding," the old man said, laughing. "I always get people with that one. Relax, you're just dreaming."

"So this isn't real?"

"Oh no, it's very real, and our time here together is going to be very important; it's just that I had to get you away from all the hustle and bustle of the world so that we could really talk, and this was the best way to do it—to come to you in a dream."

Something inside of Dominic made him believe what the old man was saying. After all, if this wasn't a dream, what he had just seen outside was really scary. He didn't know of any magician that could make the world disappear, so he must be telling the truth.

"So are you ready to continue our talk now?" the old man asked.

Dominic walked back over to Him and sat down. He looked at Him and asked, "If you're really who you say you are, why did you bother coming to me in a dream? What makes me so special that you would do that for me?"

"I come to everyone some way or another. I love you, Dominic, and I want to help you. Do you believe that?"

"Yes, Jesus, I believe you."

"Good, I'm really glad to hear that." He stood up and held out His hand to Dominic. "Come, follow me."

Chapter Thirteen

D ominic took the hand of Jesus. They walked down the side aisle in the direction of the picture they had spoken about before. He couldn't understand exactly what was happening. Jesus told him that this was just a dream, but the sight and feeling of this experience seemed very real. The feel of his hand in the hand of Jesus felt real. He could feel the grip of His hand in his. He was watching Jesus walk right next to him. It was a different kind of Jesus he had never pictured before. It wasn't that solemn-faced man hanging on the cross. This was a normal human being. He didn't speak to him in parables; He spoke to him just like any other person. He was experiencing Jesus in a way he had never dreamed of.

Dominic hadn't thought about Jesus in years, and years before that, the only time he thought of Him was when he wanted to ask for something. Why, then, was He here with Dominic now? He didn't know, but he knew he was comfortable. There was something calming about talking to someone who already knew everything about him. It was a feeling Dominic had never felt before. He had spent most of his life hiding behind the truth, never wanting anyone to know what he really was: a scared and lost young man. That sad truth didn't seem to matter, talking to Jesus. He knew exactly who Dominic was, and He had come to spend time with him knowing all his faults.

It was a hard thing to comprehend for Dominic, Jesus being a friend. It wasn't so hard to understand when he thought he was just talking to an old priest. He had gotten used to the idea that that was just one of the things priests do, try to make others feel better and deal with their problems. But now that he knew whom he was talking to, it was a little harder to understand. This Jesus came to him as a friend. He was Dominic's own personal Jesus.

The old man, Jesus, had told Dominic before that what Dominic needed to do was become friends with Jesus and let Him know what he was going through. *Maybe that's why He didn't reveal Himself sooner*, he thought. Either way, he felt honored to be able to have this talk with Him.

He didn't feel like asking any more questions or complicating the moment with thoughts in his head with why Jesus would take the time to do this. Maybe it was just like He had told Dominic before; he had just never looked for Jesus before now.

The reason didn't matter to Dominic at the moment. He would have time to think about that later. What mattered now was spending time with his new friend; however He wanted to spend the time with Dominic would be just fine with him, he decided. So instead of complicating things with questions, he just walked with his Savior.

Chapter Fourteen

As the two continued their walk along the dark hallway in the church, Jesus turned to Dominic and asked, "Do you trust me, Dominic?"

"What kind of a question is that?" Dominic said. "I am here with you now, aren't I?"

"Please answer my question."

Dominic could see Jesus's face had become strained and that He seemed pensive. He knew something was troubling Jesus, and the time for making jokes was over. He took Jesus's hand and said, "Yes, Lord, of course I trust you."

"Good, thank you."

The two continued to walk hand in hand. The hallway began to darken even more. Dominic could no longer see anything around them. "I can't see anything," Dominic said to Jesus.

"I know," Jesus said. "Just trust me."

Dominic became worried. Where was Jesus taking him? Maybe He had come to take Dominic away. Dominic's heart began to race; he broke out into a sweat. He gripped Jesus's strong hand a little tighter.

"Don't be afraid, Dominic," Jesus said. "You are safe. You are with me."

Dominic could not see anything in the distance. The darkness had become so blinding he could not even see Jesus next to him anymore. He asked, "Where are we going?"

"A place you know very well, Dominic. Don't be afraid; I won't leave your side."

Dominic could tell they weren't in the same place anymore. The feel of the floor was different; the air around him was different. He just couldn't put his finger on it. A light began to dimly shine in the distance. They approached it quickly, and it became brighter and brighter. They were walking down some sort of hallway.

The walls were made of stone. The air was stale and cold. The surroundings were all too familiar to Dominic, for he had spent the last eight years of his life in a place just like this. Why on earth would Jesus bring him back to a place like this? Dominic didn't understand.

He heard a steel door close up ahead. A guard walked toward them; his keys jingled as he walked. As he came closer, Dominic read the name of the place written on his uniform. It was the same jail they had brought him to the night of the accident. Dominic became even more confused; he turned to Jesus and asked, "Why did you bring me here?"

Jesus was no longer next to Dominic. He began to panic; he was now alone in the hallway. Why would Jesus bring him here and then leave him alone? His heart began to race. He heard a whimper come from the cell just ahead. Dominic walked closer to the door. As he approached, the sound became more and more clear. There was someone crying in the cell.

Dominic walked right up to the door and peered into the

small cell through the tiny window. There was a young man with jet-black hair on the tiny bed at the opposite end of the room. He was weeping, and he had his face in his hands.

Dominic saw Jesus's reflection join his in the small window. "Who is that in there?" he asked Jesus, but He didn't reply. He just put His arm around Dominic.

The young man stood up and walked toward the small sink in the room. As he rose to his feet, his eyes met Dominic's. The pain on his face was unmistakable. It was as if Dominic was looking in the mirror, for the young man in the room was him.

Dominic's heart sank, his knees became weak, and he leaned against Jesus. No words came to mind; he just continued to watch the young man as he walked over to the sink and splashed some water on his face. The young man looked at himself in the mirror; he clinched his teeth. His face now had an expression of pain and anger, a look of sadness and self-hate, as he stared himself in the face. He punched the stone wall beside the mirror. He began to pace back and forth in the room.

Dominic began to feel the loneliness, pain, and anger of that night well up inside of him. He felt a tear well up in his right eye and trickle down his face as he watched his young self in the room.

"Are you okay?" Jesus asked.

"No, I'm not okay," Dominic shouted at Jesus as he shoved Him away. "Why couldn't you have come to me that night? How could you sit up there on your high horse watching me and the pain I was in and do nothing? Don't you see the agony I'm going through in there? You say you want to be friends?

Why should I trust you when you watched me go through the hardest moment of my life and did nothing?"

"I was right there with you," Jesus said quietly, "every moment."

"Oh yeah?" Dominic shouted. "Well, you coulda fooled me, 'cause I sure don't remember you being there that night. I had never felt more alone in my entire life than I did that night."

"Take another look in the room, Dominic."

"No. I don't want to relive that night anymore."

"There's something you need to see," Jesus said.

Dominic looked into the room again. The young man was now on his knees, weeping in the middle of the room. Dominic looked at Jesus. "You know what I'm doing there?" Jesus said nothing. "I'm praying, and a lot of good that did me, huh?" Dominic said sarcastically.

"Well, you've seen this moment through your eyes; now look at them through mine," Jesus said.

"What do you mean, through your eyes?"

"Have another look and see what I mean."

Dominic looked into the room again; he was still in the middle of the room on his knees, praying on the cement floor. The scene had another character this time, however; there was another man in the room with him, kneeling in front of him with both of his hands on Dominic's shoulders. Dominic watched as the man stroked Dominic's shoulders. The man was crying with Dominic. He pressed Dominic to his chest and held him as the two cried together. The man glanced at Dominic in the window with tears in his eyes.

"Do you recognize the man with you in there?" Jesus asked.

"Yeah," Dominic said, a little choked up by the tenderness of the scene. "It's you."

Chapter Fifteen

I told you that I was with you the whole time, Dominic," Jesus said. "I would never lie to you."

"I know you wouldn't," Dominic said, "but why did I feel so alone that night?"

"There was something for you to learn that night."

"What?"

"That night taught you how it feels to be alone," Jesus said. "That night taught you what it feels like to lose everything: the life of your best friend and your own life. Because even though you didn't know it at the time, after that night, your life was never going to be the same. That night gave you a heart that can understand and sympathize with others who are going through a tough time, and as hard as it was for me to see you going through so much pain, that same pain is what will allow you to do my work the rest of your time on earth."

If He knew it was for my benefit, why was it hard for Him to watch? "Why was it hard for you to see me go through that?"

"Because I've felt that way myself. I know what it's like to feel completely alone and abandoned. I know what it's like to feel like everybody has left you, and I hated seeing you go through that. You are my friend; you are my son. And there is nothing more painful for a father to see than to watch his son go through such pain."

This didn't make any sense to Dominic. How could God feel alone? "You've felt that way before?" Dominic asked.

"Oh yes," Jesus said. "I've had almost the exact same feelings you did that night."

"When?"

"Come with me and I'll show you," Jesus said, holding out His hand to Dominic.

Dominic took the hand of Jesus, and the two began walking down the hallway back toward the dark, leaving the two men weeping in the room together. The two walked down the hallway until they were in complete darkness again. "Where are we going now?" Dominic asked Jesus through the darkness.

"Well, I got to experience your darkest hour with you," Jesus said. "Now I'm going to share my darkest hour with you."

"What do you mean?"

"Take my hand. I'll show you."

Chapter Sixteen

The two continued down the same dark, unlit hallway they came in through, hand in hand. Dominic wasn't sure where they were headed to, but at this point, he was sure that no matter where it was they were going, Jesus would not leave his side.

As they walked, Dominic began to notice that the ground had changed underneath his feet. They were now walking on gravel. Where on earth could they be?

Before Dominic had time to ponder the idea of where Jesus could be taking him, he began to hear yelling and weeping coming from the end of the hallway, which now had a dim light at the end of it.

Dominic ran his hand along the wall of the hallway. He felt cold, moist stone underneath his fingertips. The stones were rough and unfinished, sort of like the side of a hill or the inside of a cave. This was obviously unfamiliar territory to Dominic; the only time he had been in a place like this was on vacation. Suddenly Dominic felt a jolt of energy enter his body, like he and Jesus were about to have some kind of adventure.

The shouts and cries became louder as they approached the mouth of the tunnel. Dominic could now feel the heat of the air outside the tunnel. It was sunny out, and the light was almost blinding as they stepped outside. As Dom's eyes adjusted, he felt sweat begin to build up on his forehead.

As his eyes began to focus, he realized that he was in a place unlike he had ever seen before. There was a mob of people around, all dressed as though they were from the Middle East, with long robes and some kind of turbans wrapped on their heads. They were dressed as if they were straight out of a storybook; however, not a happy story was taking place. Some people in the crowd were crying out loud, and some were shouting in fury.

From where he was standing, he had a good view of the crowd beneath him. Although they were spread out over a good distance, they seemed to be moving in a general direction, and many of them moved in a tight bunch. Dominic turned to Jesus to ask Him where He had taken him this time, but just as before, He had temporarily taken physical leave from beside Dominic.

Dominic decided to get a better look at what was going on, so he headed toward the center of the mob. As he got closer to the center, he had to push and shove his way through the people. Whatever it was they were shouting, Dominic could not understand them; they were speaking some language he had never heard before. But the looks on their faces told him enough.

Dominic fought his way almost to the front of the mob, and he could see what the commotion was about now. There was a man stumbling his way down the stone-covered dirt path. Some of the people were throwing things at him as they shouted.

Who was this guy that the people hated so much? Dominic had to get to the front of the pack to get a better look at this guy; best he could make out, he must be some criminal. Again, Dominic went to pushing his way through the crowd, and soon he was at the front and center of the action. The man was hunched over because of the wooden object he was carrying, a cross.

"No way. It couldn't be, could it?" Dominic said to himself. The man fell in front of Dominic with his hand landing right at Dominic's feet. Dominic recognized that suntanned, muscular hand, and when the man looked up at him, there was no mistaking him anymore. It was Jesus, beaten worse than anyone Dominic had ever seen before. Blood ran down the front of His face, His eyes full of pain and fear. He looked desperately to Dominic as if He wanted him to do something, but what could Dominic do?

Jesus struggled to get up under the weight of the cross and immediately fell down. Dominic felt so scared. He wanted to help Jesus so badly but was afraid of the Roman soldiers guarding Jesus.

Jesus looked up at Dominic again in despair. Dominic felt hopeless. What could he do to help his friend? Just then, someone shoved him from behind. Dominic looked back at the man who had shoved him with hands open and a confused look on his face, as if to ask, "What was that for?"

Evidently the man understood because he pointed behind Dominic at something. Dominic turned around and saw a Roman soldier sitting on a big, black, armored horse. He pointed to Dominic with his sword and then pointed toward Jesus.

Dominic pointed to himself as if to say, "You want me to help Him?" The soldier yelled at Dominic as another came and threw him on the ground next to Jesus.

Well, I guess that was a yes. Now Dominic had no choice; whether he wanted to or not, he was going to be helping his new friend for the rest of the way, he figured. As Dominic began to rise to his feet, his eyes met Jesus's eyes. A glance was all it took for a short conversation to occur between the two of them. Jesus's eyes said to Dominic, "Thanks a lot, buddy."

Dominic's eyes replied, "Don't worry; I'm here till the end, just like you are for me."

Dominic picked up the cross and let Jesus throw His arm around him, and the two once again continued on their walk together.

Chapter Seventeen

The weight of the cross and Jesus was nearly overwhelming to Dominic as he lugged his friend and the terrible torture device He was made to carry. The muscles in his legs burned as he placed one foot in front of the other down the dirt path. Dominic could hear Jesus breathing heavily in his ear; it sounded as if He were struggling just to breathe at that point.

Dominic couldn't understand how Jesus could continue, given the condition He was in. Dominic had only carried the cross a fraction of the way, and he was already extremely tired. He could only imagine how Jesus felt physically. He looked as though He had been beaten severely. He had deep cuts all the way down the front of His body and His back—oh, His back; it looked as though someone had tried to superglue random pieces of flesh onto Him. A piece here, a piece there, and every piece seemed to be hanging on by just a thread. His blood trickled on the ground underneath them. It seemed as though every beat of His heart was sending blood onto the ground instead of into His body. How could He possibly be enduring this?

Dominic's thoughts were interrupted by a groan let out by Jesus. Dominic wished he could tell his friend that it would be okay, that they were almost there, but he knew how this story ended. He knew things were just going to get far worse and that everything would not be okay. They were now making their way up a pretty good-sized hill. Off in the distance, Dominic could see there was already a large crowd gathered at the top of the hill.

Jesus let out a cough as He cleared His throat and turned to Dominic and said, "You know, if you're going to be my friend, you are going to have to do this every day for the rest of your life."

"What?" Dominic asked in complete confusion. "What are you talking about?"

"I mean that, for the rest of your life," Jesus struggled with every word, "you will have to pick up your cross every day, just like today, and follow me."

"You know, I don't think my body could handle doing this every day."

"I don't necessarily mean physically, though some of the trials you face may be physical, whether it is an injury or an illness you have to endure and overcome. There are many other crosses you will be asked to carry as you follow in my ways."

"What kind of crosses are you talking about?" Dominic asked. "How hard is this going to be exactly?"

"There are many sorts of trials you will have to face in your life, as you already know, and you have already faced many trials in your time here thus far," Jesus said. "Crosses come in the form of these trials. Some have to deal with and overcome an addiction of some kind; others have to deal with the loss of a loved one. Still others have to deal with some sort of physical ailment. But no matter what type of cross you may be given to carry at different points in your life, know that I am with you, helping you every step of the way, just as you are here helping me now."

Jesus's breathing became more labored, and to Dominic, it seemed as if He let more and more of His weight rest on him with every step. The words Jesus said gave Dominic some concern. Was something really bad about to happen in his life? "Why are you telling me this? Are you trying to scare me or something?"

Jesus let out a painful sounding half grunt, half laugh and said, "No, I'm not trying to scare you. I just want you to know that just because you live your life according to my words, it doesn't mean that it will be a walk in the park."

"Well, that doesn't seem fair, if you ask me," Dominic said. "You are asking me to be a better person, a person different from who I was before, a person different from what the world may expect me to be, and you're telling me that for all my work and sacrifice, my grand reward is more trials and more suffering? You don't make this lifestyle sound so appealing. It's a good thing you weren't a salesman, 'cause I don't think you could have made a living doing that."

Jesus let out a painful sounding chuckle. "Well, keep in mind you are not working for an earthly reward; you will be repaid greatly in the next life if you follow my ways."

"Okay, that sounds better," Dominic said.

Dominic's thoughts quickly returned to the condition his friend was in. Jesus was now almost draped around Dominic like a towel, His head resting gently on Dominic's chest. The thorns from His crown dug into Dominic's chest; the pain was uncomfortable but not overwhelming. Besides, how could he complain when his friend was in such a poor condition? Dominic's steps now became almost as deliberate as Jesus's breathing. The weight of Jesus and the cross now almost felt overwhelming. He didn't know if he would be able to make the last few hundred yards up the hill.

Just as soon as the thought of doubt that he would be able to make it came into his mind, Jesus whispered quietly to him, "Don't worry, my son; we are almost there."

The words quickly drew a bag of mixed emotions for Dominic. Even though the load he carried was heavy, he knew that once his job was done, it would only be the beginning of Jesus's great suffering on the cross. He suddenly wanted to turn around, pick Jesus up, and run away from there to someplace safe, someplace where he could tend to his friend and nurse Him back to health. The thoughts began to overwhelm Dominic; he stopped walking as he pondered the idea.

As if to answer the questions bouncing back and forth in his head, Jesus said, "Sometimes the trials we face in this life are daunting. They seem as if the price that has to be paid for the reward is too expensive, but I assure you that if the cause is just, it will be worth the fight."

Dominic knew that those words were not coincidental. He knew that Jesus spoke them as words of encouragement to ease his doubts, and he knew he had no other choice than to continue on the last few hundred feet.

The two friends were now nearing their destination. Dominic felt as if he were walking in quicksand now. His steps were short and painful. As Dominic took those last few strides, Jesus turned to him and said, "I want you to know that it means a lot to me, the effort that you have put into this. And I want you to know that no matter what you face in this life, I will be there to help you, just like you have helped me here. No matter what the trial or tribulation, you can count on me. I will be your friend when no one else is there. I will be your strength when you can't stand, and I will be your guide when you are lost. All you have to do is call for me, and I will be there, because you are my friend, you are my son, and I love you."

Dominic was so moved by Jesus that tears began to well up in his eyes. He wanted to say something; he wanted to cry out loud; he wanted to tell Jesus how much this walk they had taken meant to Him. But as he held Jesus for those last few seconds, the first words that came to mind were the only words that he could get out. "I love you," Dominic said through his tears.

Just then, a crashing blow landed on the back of Dominic's neck. As the two fell under the weight of the cross and the blow, Jesus's crown of thorns dug deeply into Dominic's chest and cut him. As they fell to the ground, Dominic began to drift out of consciousness, for the blow the soldier dealt was severe.

As Dominic hit the ground, his eyes met Jesus's eyes one last time. Dominic had never seen more love in another's eyes before. He wanted to look into those eyes forever; he wanted that moment to last, but just as soon as the moment came, it was gone. And it was dark.

Chapter Eighteen

Dominic awoke to a nudge on his shoulder. He had a headache; his head rested on a hard wood of some sort. It was a struggle to open his eyes, so he kept them closed as he sat up.

"Dominic," a familiar voice said to him.

Without looking to see who it was, he said, "Yeah, Mom."

"Dominic, what are you doing here? This is the last place I expected to find you."

"Yeah, well, I came here to get in out of the rain and ended up staying a little longer than I expected. Sorry I missed my homecoming dinner. I must have fallen asleep."

"You didn't miss anything," his mom said. "It's still the middle of the afternoon."

"What?" Dominic asked. "Well, then why did you come looking for me if I wasn't late yet?"

"I didn't come looking for you. I was out running some last-minute errands before dinner, and I ran into an older gentleman as I was walking to my car. He said I could find you in here."

"Well, what time is it?"

"Oh, it must be a little after three by now. You look like you had a good nap."

"Yeah, sorta," Dominic said as he sat up and rubbed his eyes. He looked down at his watch. The time read 3:16. Dominic chuckled.

"What's so funny?" she asked.

"Oh, nothing."

"Oh, well, I'm so glad to see you in some normal clothes again," his mom said. "You look so handsome."

His mom was already ready with a compliment for him. Dominic knew that it was a mother's opinion of her son, but it made him feel good regardless. "Thanks, Ma," Dominic said.

"I'm sure everyone else will be excited to see you. They are all waiting for you at the house already."

The nervousness about seeing his family now seemed like a distant memory to Dominic. He was no longer nervous but excited to see his family. "Yeah, well, I can't wait to see them either."

"So what do you say?" she asked. "You wanna go home?"

"Yeah, that sounds like just what the doctor ordered," Dominic said as he stood up and put his arm around his mom. They started walking toward the back of the church.

As they neared the big wooden doors of the back of the church, Dom's mom turned to him and said, "Ouchy."

"What?" Dominic asked. "Why did you say that?"

"You cut yourself and tore your shirt. We're gonna have to get that taken care of when we get home."

I thought He said that was just a dream? Dominic thought. *I guess some dreams are more real than we'd like to think.* Dominic chuckled as he opened the wooden door and said, "Okay, Ma, you're the boss." And as his mom walked through the open door, he looked back at the large cross with the body of Jesus hanging at the front of the church and said, "Thanks, thanks for everything."

"Who are you talking to?" his mom asked.

"Oh, just a friend."

The two walked down the cement steps and toward her car. "And what were you doing at church anyway?" she questioned him. "You were never big on church."

"Man, you ask a lot of questions," Dominic said. "Reminds me of someone else I know."

"Well, I'm your mother," she said as they got into the car. "I'm allowed to ask questions. So what were you doing in there?"

"Oh, not too much. Just had a little talk with Jesus."

Epilogue

Dominic's mom handed a plate of freshly made hamburger patties through the kitchen window for Dominic to cook on the grill. "Are you sure we need these many burgers, Mom?" Dominic asked as he took the plate and placed it next to the grill.

"I am expecting quite a few people today, and I don't want them to go hungry," his mom replied as she came back with some brats and hot dogs and handed them to Dominic. "Here, throw those on too, hon."

"Okay, just let me ask you this," Dominic said, a hint of humor in his tone.

"And what's that?" his mom replied, looking intently at her son.

"Why am I cooking for my own party?"

"Your dad and I paid for the schooling and the food. I figured you could at least cook," his mom said, a big grin drawn on her face.

"Okay, I can't argue with that." Dominic turned to face the charcoal grill, which had now surrounded the backyard with the scent of hamburgers. *I don't know what I would have done without my parents*, Dominic thought. *They've done more for me than I could ever repay them for.* "Thank you," he said, shooting a glance toward the sky.

After Dominic had found Christ that day in St. Patrick's Church, his life was never the same again. As drastically as Dominic's life had changed for the worse after the accident, that's how much better it was now. He felt better than ever, and it showed. No longer was Dominic a quiet, selfish, and angry man who walked around with a chip on his shoulder. No, the new Dominic cared for others and wore a smile on his face. He loved his family; he loved life.

"Smells good, pal," Dominic's dad said as he walked through the door to the backyard.

"Thanks, Dad," Dominic said as he scooped a burger off the grill and placed it in a container to stay warm.

"Can I get you anything?"

"Just a chance for me to thank you for making this day possible," Dominic said as he set the spatula down and turned to face his dad. "Thanks for everything." Dominic embraced his dad.

"I love you, Dominic," his dad said as they embraced. "I'm proud of the way you have changed your life."

"Thanks, Dad," Dominic said, fighting back a tear. "I love you too."

"If Dominic's doing the cooking, we're all in trouble," Evan said as he made his usual grand entrance. "How ya doing, buddy?" He walked over to Dominic, reaching out his hand to greet him.

"I'm good, buddy," Dominic said as they pulled each other

in and gave each other a slap on the back. "Thanks for coming."

"Wouldn't miss it," Evan said. "I'm proud of you, man. Look at you. You have it all, and now you can add college graduate to the list."

"Thanks," Dominic said with a big smile on his face.

"Somebody was missing his daddy," Christina said as she walked over to Dominic, holding the greatest gift Dominic had ever been given. "He wanted to come see you." She passed their newborn son to Dominic.

"Hey, honey," Dominic said as he simultaneously took the newborn from her arms and gave her a gentle kiss. "Hey, Eddy. How's daddy's little boy?"

"I'm jealous," Evan said, smiling. "You got it all. Great wife, great family, and a new son!"

Dominic kissed his son on the forehead and said, "It's amazing how the big guy upstairs can change your life with just a little talk."